LUNA RISING

BOOK 1 OF THE LUNA RISING SERIES (A PARANORMAL SHIFTER ROMANCE SERIES)

SARA SNOW

RUBY

*L*ife is finally about to stop kicking me in the ass, and the world is going to know my name. Everything is about to change.

I repeated my morning affirmation three more times as I exited the cab and looked around at my new school. I am in college. I, Ruby Saunders, have made it to college. I'll still have to work my ass off to maintain my grades and qualify for my full ride, of course, but nothing is going to deter me from my path. I've worked too long and too hard to get where I am now, so all distractions can go to hell. I'm not saying I won't attend the occasional party, but I know the opportunity I've been given will be gone forever if I lose it. I can't pay for college on my own; I can barely pay for lunch.

"Damn babe, nice ass."

My eyes narrowed as I stopped walking. I sighed as I turned around while pulling my hands out of the pockets of my leather jacket. The distractions were starting earlier than I had expected, and I wasn't in the mood. Five minutes. Only five minutes had passed on my first day, and I already had this to deal with.

Sure enough, there was a boy behind me eyeing me up and down, his bright blue eyes twinkling with lust. I tilted my head to the side and smiled, and his face lit up even further. He wasn't bad looking, but he was a distraction and I wasn't about to be his next victim.

"What did you just say to me, you little bitch?" I said. His eyes widened as I raised a finger to his face. "Shut the fuck up."

"Ahh, I…"

I turned away before he could spit out whatever it was he was trying to say while behind him, his friends started laughing. I know what you're thinking, I didn't have to be that mean. But if you knew the life I've lived, you'd understand my determination to stay focused, which meant no boys.

For most of my life – almost all of it actually – I've been alone. I've been looking after myself for as long as I can remember, and that's how it will continue to be. People like me don't get offered help. Nor do we need it. I can take care of myself.

After leaving the admissions office a little earlier than I had expected, I decided to do a tour of the school. My first class wouldn't be starting for another hour, so I had some time to kill.

There was a dark academy aesthetic about this place that I knew I'd never grow tired of. From the moment I had seen this place online, I knew this was where I was meant to be. So, after receiving my scholarship, I packed up what little I had (which fit into one suitcase), pocketed my last three hundred bucks, and came here.

I inhaled deeply as the wind picked up and whipped my hair around me, the red strands tangling around my face. The buildings were all of a gothic design with vines going up the walls. People mostly spoke in hushed voices, and with the sky being overcast, the campus was shrouded in darkness.

I was at home.

Sometimes in life, you'll get a feeling in your gut, a feeling that pushes you to do or say something, and more often than not you end up living with regret if you ignore it. So far, I'm happy I took the risk of coming here.

The library is hands down my favorite place here. The quiet that greets you along with the slightly musty air gives you the feeling you've stepped into another world. As soon as I stepped inside I was inundated with the smell of old books, and my heart rate sped up. Victorian style lamps lining the walls and a giant chandelier hanging from the ceiling provided soft lighting that left shadows all over the library.

I made my way through the shelves, taking deep breaths as I glided my fingers along the spines of the books.

Oh yes, I'd be spending a lot of time here, a lot of time indeed.

Ever since childhood, books have been my way out, my escape from the shitty reality I live in. One day something I've written will offer someone a means of escape. Yeah, I know, weird idea since I'm a law major.

I had exited the shelves upon shelves of books to take a seat when, a few tables away from me, a guy got to his feet.

It was like watching a giant who had been crouching down stand tall. The man before me was at least six foot four with raven black hair, a square sharp jawline, and perfectly shaped thick brows. He was looking around the library and, if his knitted brows were anything to go by, he was angry.

Maybe he had been waiting on someone and they had stood him up. But who would stand up a guy like that? He was clearly a gym junkie, with one of his arms as big as my two arms combined.

As the man began to walk away, I heard a voice behind me. "He's hot, isn't he?"

I looked over my shoulder to see a girl bent down to my ear level, her blue eyes glistening with amusement. "Don't waste your time, honey. Every woman on this campus wants a piece of him, and he gives none of them the time of day."

Who was this girl and why was she talking to me? She had caught me checking that guy out, whoever he was. So what? Was she a jealous ex or something?

"Um, okay. Don't worry, I'm not interested."

Her eyes widened as if I had said the world was flat before a grin pulled at her lips, and she sat down. "Hmm, how interesting. I get the vibe you don't run with the crowd. That's good." She stuck her hand out to me. "I'm Natalie."

I shook her hand because, why not? She seemed nice. "Ruby."

"Fitting name, Ruby, with your red hair and all." She squinted and leaned closer. "A natural redhead at that. Nice!"

Now I wouldn't say I'm the most beautiful woman to walk the earth, but my hair has always drawn attention to me, both its color and the fact that it reaches below my ass. And the bangs that stop just above my eyebrows make my small oval face appear smaller. I'm five foot five, have decent C-cup boobs, and I have some curvy hips. Hence, the comment I had gotten from that poor guy earlier.

Natalie, however, was a model. I've never been the type to be jealous of another woman's looks, but Natalie was tall, five foot seven at least, with legs like a gazelle and platinum blonde hair. Her ice-blue eyes were the icing on the cake.

"Yup. So who was that guy then?"

She smirked. "Oh, so you *are* interested?"

"I'm curious," I corrected her. "Only curious."

And that was the truth, because he *was* hot. Gorgeous even. He was tall and muscular, and while he was extremely handsome, there was an aura of seriousness about him that I liked.

She exhaled and looked in the direction he had gone. "He's Xavier Blackwood, son of Mathieu Blackwood." She looked over at me and smiled. "Xavier is part of the rich-kids crowd, although he rolls alone. That actually makes girls want him more. I'm not sure if it's a trick or not, but there you have it. You can try your luck, sis."

"I'll pass, *sis*."

She shrugged, not in the least bothered by my snappy response, and I found myself liking her. Looking at her, you'd think she'd be a materialistic "oh my god I, like, so need a skinny latte" type, but she seemed rather chill.

I can't stand a calorie-watching bitch. Eat food!

I checked my watch, and my eyes widened. I couldn't believe my hour was almost up. I got up and picked up my bag. "Hey, sorry, but I have class. I can't miss my first class."

She got up with me. "Sure, what building are you going to?"

"Law."

She grinned. "Nice, so am I. Let's go. You can tell me how you've managed to get an ass like that."

I laughed, and she winked at me as we left.

Yeah, I like her. That makes my first day a success because I usually can't stand people in general.

Ruby

The day I had arrived in town I started job hunting. Mind you, by then I was down to two hundred bucks and still needed to find a place to stay. But my determination has always gotten me through, and finally, the fourth diner I visited needed someone immediately. For my job interview, all I had to do was serve customers for an hour. With my years of experience waiting tables (since it's the only job I've ever been able to keep), I landed the job easily.

My supervisor knew someone who knew someone who had just moved out of their broom closet apartment, and I was more than happy to take it. Now, two weeks later and with school started, I felt like my life was slowly coming together.

I'd even made a friend.

"Thanks, Ruby," a regular said to me. The old man tipped me twenty bucks. "This place needed a pretty face like yours."

"I heard that Mr. Jackson, and I take offense."

Mr. Jackson flipped Brittany off. She's my coworker and the only other employee besides my supervisor. She laughed and went back to cleaning the tables. She's Goth, with a million piercings in each ear. And even though our supervisor Rosette keeps telling her to stop wearing black lipstick,

Brittany would wear it anyway and say it's not lipstick, it's her natural lip color.

Everything was going great until Natalie walked in, and I nearly had a stroke when I saw who was walking in behind her.

Xavier Blackwood strutted into the diner like he owned the place and took a seat. With him was a girl who was giving everyone the stink eye, her brown hair in a slick high pony-tail, and a guy with curly blonde hair who looked extremely bored.

"Hey, gorgeous," Natalie called to me as she glided over to the counter I was leaning on. She plucked a cookie out of the jar beside me and winked at Brittany, who to my surprise started blushing.

Strange.

"Don't 'hey gorgeous' me! Explain. You're part of that crowd?"

Natalie glanced over at her shoulder. "Oh. Well, that crowd is my family. Xavier's my cousin."

What the fuck did she just say?

"Excuse me? You called him hot."

"Yeah, I know."

"He's your cousin, Natalie. No one calls their cousin hot."

She ate the last of the cookie and grinned. "I was only voicing what you were thinking. Anyway, what time do you get off?"

"First of all, I wasn't thinking that. And I'm doing a double shift tonight."

She pouted, but it only lasted a second. "Fine, I just wanted the guys to try the burgers here. If it wasn't for you, I wouldn't have known they were so good."

She kissed my cheek and pranced over to Xavier and friends. I stood there, rooted to my spot. I wasn't bothered by her kissing my cheek. I've only known her for two days, but it feels like I've known her for decades. Her cheery personality is hard to dislike.

What had me rooted to the spot was Xavier's eyes. They were like black pits and they were trained on me. Why was he staring at me, and why did he look upset?

His brows were so tightly knit I figured he was going to get a headache soon. The girl he had come in with didn't like his attention being elsewhere. She threw her hand over his shoulder and began whispering to him, but her eyes were on me.

Oh honey, if only you knew how much I *don't* want Xavier Blackwood.

My brows pulled together as I turned away and placed my hand over my heart. My heart rate had spiked, and a horrible feeling was rolling up my chest. I coughed, but that had been a mistake.

"Um, Brittany, I'm taking a break."

My chest was burning, and I felt light-headed. I could feel the vomit making its way up my throat. What the hell is happening? I don't get sick, ever. I've caught the flu probably only twice since I was a child.

I turned and headed for the door, passing Natalie's table.

"Ruby?"

"I'm taking my break, Natalie. Someone else will take your order."

She got to her feet as if to follow me outside, a look of worry plastered on her face, but the other guy, the one who looked bored, grabbed her arm. I didn't care because the world around me was starting to tilt. As I ran outside, I held onto the wall and threw up until I fell to my knees.

Ruby

𝓡osette gave me an hour break, instead of fifteen minutes. I stared up at the ceiling in the office where I'd been lying down for that hour. I've never thrown up so much in my life, but the feeling was almost gone. With my stomach now empty, I felt drained of all my energy.

I tried to remember what I had eaten that could have made me sick, but all I've had since this morning was a sandwich and then a muffin when I got to work. Maybe what I needed was a proper meal.

I grimaced. The thought of food was making me feel sick again, and I decided with the feeling passing I'd better get back to work. Rosette had argued with me for ten minutes that I should go home, but I need the money. My scholarship covers my school expenses, but I still have to eat.

I made my way back into the diner to take over from Brittany when my eyes landed on Xavier.

What was he still doing here?

He was alone but sitting in the exact spot he had been before. He looked up as I was putting my apron on and his eyes lowered into slits. My hands froze from tying my apron as his face morphed from relaxed to angry.

What in God's name did I do to this man?

I've only seen him once before, that day in the library. And considering that I'm friends with Natalie, what reason does he have for looking at me as if I'm a plague beast? Did Natalie tell him what I had said, that I wasn't interested in him, and he's somehow upset about it? That was the only thing I could think of, but I wasn't going to stand around and have this creep watch me my whole shift.

"Can I help you with something? Why do you keep staring at me?"

Xavier looked up at me and my heart lodged itself in my throat when he abruptly got to his feet, his nostrils flaring. I backed up, my eyes widening as his narrowed even further. My head was tilted back because of how he was towering over me, and just like that, I was hit with another wave of nausea.

My face twisted in pain, and he recoiled from me.

Was that it? Was he repulsed by me being sick or something? Jesus, what is with this guy? But God, was he even more perfect up close. I still didn't like him. Why is he acting like this? For a second there, I thought he was going to hit me.

He turned and stormed out of the diner, everyone having frozen to watch the scene.

"Do you know Xavier Blackwood?"

I looked over at Brittany and inhaled a breath. Throwing up even once more would surely kill me. "No. I don't know what his problem is."

She threw me a look I couldn't decipher before turning away to clock out for the day. From what I understood, Xavier's father was Mathieu Blackwood, the business mogul and millionaire. They were among the elite, and considering I was new in town, there was no reason for this man to hate me.

By the time the last customer left, I was again on the verge of fainting. I had munched on a few cookies throughout the night, but what I needed was rest. With tomorrow being Sunday and since my Monday assignments were already completed, I could sleep in.

I closed up the diner and zipped my jacket as the chilly air nipped at my skin. In the distance, I could hear music, no doubt from a bar or club or frat house nearby. Since my apartment was close by, many nights I walked home instead of calling an Uber. It's the only exercise I get since I've never seen the inside of a gym.

Xavier's face flashed in my mind, and I rolled my eyes. Something was seriously wrong with that guy, and you could bet on Monday I'd confront him for it. His father could be the president, I didn't care. You don't get to do stuff like that and walk.

My eyes narrowed and my steps slowed when before me, a man in a hoodie pushed himself off a wall and turned in my direction. He just stood there staring at me, his face cloaked in darkness with his hoodie pulled over his head.

Shit.

I turned around, but a chill ran down my spine when behind me was another man.

Oh, Jesus.

I turned and walked briskly down an alleyway, my hand rummaging through my handbag. I closed my eyes and cursed inwardly, my heart pounding in my head as I realized I'd left my pepper spray at home.

Behind me, I heard a whistle and another man appeared before me. No, no, this was not happening right now. This wasn't happening! Two weeks, I've been here for two weeks! My life was turning around! I got a scholarship!

The most gruesome thoughts started going through my head. I turned to run, but my way out of the alleyway was blocked by the first two men. They charged at me, grabbing both my arms and holding them apart.

"Hey, babe," the man who had appeared in the alleyway whispered, his voice low and gravelly. My skin started to crawl as he reached a finger out and ran it down my cheek. "Why are you walking home alone, princess?"

"I like to stretch my legs." I kicked him in the gut, sending him staggering backward. At the same time, I yanked on my arms, but only one came free. Before I knew it, the two men had grabbed me again. This time, one of them held my face, squeezing my cheeks.

The man before me started laughing and removed his hood, revealing a deep scar running down the side of his face. His skin was pale and his breath reeked of alcohol. I wanted to cry. My eyes were stinging, and I knew what was coming next when he smiled at me.

"I love 'em feisty."

My world started crumbling when he started grabbing at me, his cold fingers prying at my body until I felt them, like ice cubes, dip into my top and grab my breast. I screamed. I screamed for my life, for someone to save me, when suddenly the man to my left was yanked away.

I slapped my attacker in the face and pushed the other away but it proved unnecessary. They had already forgotten about me because, behind us, their friend was suspended in the air.

His neck snapped to the side with a sickening sound that

echoed in the darkness around us. I couldn't believe what I was seeing. What man has the strength to hold another off the ground like that?

The body was thrown to the side, and I got my answer as Xavier stepped forward.

2

RUBY

J think I've fallen into some alternate reality where a man who looks exactly like Xavier can hold a grown man off the ground like he's a doll.

"What the fuck did you just do?" the man to my right yelled, but he made no move towards his friend lying on the ground, his eyes open but lifeless.

I swallowed and backed up as my attacker, the sick piece of shit who had had his hand down my top, whipped out a knife. "You're going to pay for that! You're a dead fucking man!"

"Do you really think so?" Xavier asked. It was the first I'd ever heard his voice. It tickled my skin like a feather's stroke, but it also made me feel faint. I narrowed my eyes, for his voice was also softer than I had expected. He sounded so calm, so collected, for a man who had just committed murder. "Leave."

The man to my right pulled his hoodie down, revealing a bald head, and he too whipped out a knife. "We're not leaving, but you are. You're going to the fucking afterlife for what you just did, freak!"

Xavier's head tilted to the side. "I wasn't speaking to you." His eyes drifted to me, and my body went rigid. "Leave," he repeated.

My eyes widened as his dark brown irises, almost black, began to bleed into the whites of his eyes. His eyeballs turned entirely black, and a chill went down my spine that had nothing to do with the cold air. I started to sweat because he suddenly seemed taller and more muscular. But I wasn't going to let him order me to leave.

"What the…"

"Go!" he barked at me, and my body jumped as I stepped back. His teeth had elongated so much that his canines were touching the bottom of his lower lip.

The men on either side of me started backing up as well, their eyes wide with fear, as Xavier took a step forward. I swallowed, suddenly feeling the urge to piss myself, as his fingers began to twitch before black nails pierced through his cuticles. On second thought, maybe I would follow that order.

"What the fuck are you?" the man to my right said, his voice shaking, and Xavier raised his head, his nostrils flaring.

"The man who's going to make you wish you had picked another woman to fuck with."

This wasn't Xavier. I'd really stepped into an alternate universe or a fucking horror show! The man before me was a demon, a creature, a beast! He wasn't human, he wasn't Xavier!

I screamed as Xavier rushed forward, a deep growl vibrating up from his chest. I pressed my back against the wall. I watched in horror as he held onto the man's arm, the one that was holding the knife and the hand that had been down my shirt, and ripped it from his body.

I gagged, my nearly empty stomach wanting me to vomit the two cookies I had managed to keep down, as I watched Xavier throw the man's arm to the side, blood flying everywhere. He opened his mouth and sank his fangs into the man's throat, and my legs started moving.

I could hear the man's horrible screams as I ran from the alleyway. I closed my eyes for just a second as I heard the other man start to scream as well. I could hear the sound of breaking bones. I don't want to sound ungrateful for being saved, but I think I would have preferred being raped and left alone because now I'm about to be eaten alive!

What the hell kind of town did I move to?

I wanted to cry, scream, and curl up into a ball. I wanted an explanation for what I had just witnessed because, as terrified as I was, that was still the coolest thing I've ever seen in my life.

No, not the killing. That was surely going to scar me for life. But Xavier, what the hell is he?

The screaming abruptly stopped, but I kept pumping my legs, the mouth of the alleyway just before me. But I didn't get far, oh how I didn't get far, because the moment I screamed to hail a passing cab, a hand made its way around my mouth. I was out cold in the next second.

Ruby

I rolled onto my side and frowned, surprised I wasn't greeted with a view of the sky. I got out of bed sluggishly and pulled my curtain back, the way I always keep it. I wasn't a morning person. To get myself out of bed, all I need is to see the sky.

I sighed and rubbed at my eyes before looking down at the street below, my eyes following a couple as they strolled by hand in hand.

Cute couple, I thought to myself as my stomach began to growl loudly, like an animal was in there. I wasn't hungry, I was *starving*. I dragged myself to the bathroom to brush my teeth and tame my hair before making my way to the kitchen. I wasn't sure why I felt so tired or so hungry, but the sooner I had food in my system the better. I already felt like shit and didn't want to risk getting a headache.

"Oh my God!" I clutched at my chest as I walked in on Natalie sitting at my tiny island. "What the hell are you doing in my kitchen? How did you even get in?"

Natalie raised a brow. "Your door was open. I've been calling you all day. You missed class."

"What?" I looked away and frowned. "What do you mean I missed class? It's Sunday."

Her eyes narrowed at me. "Ruby, it's Monday. I've been calling you since yesterday, which was Sunday, and then all day today. I was worried about you, and your ass has been sleeping all this time."

What the hell was she saying? There was no way I'd been sleeping for two days. I held my head and sat down and she slid her mug, rather my mug, toward me.

"Have some coffee. You look like shit. What happened to you?"

I sipped the coffee and sighed. I wish I had an answer for her, but I was busy trying to understand how I had slept for two days. Why was I still so tired then? I pressed my fingers to my temples and peeped at her from under my lashes.

"Sorry I missed your calls. I must have been more tired than I thought after work on Saturday." My eyes widened. "Speaking of Saturday, your creepy ass cousin attacked me."

Natalie blinked slowly. "Xavier attacked you? Attacked you how?"

"In the diner. And he didn't literally attack me. He was staring at me, so I asked him what his problem was, and he, I don't know, reacted. I thought he was going to hit me."

Natalie looked away, her brows furrowed in thought. "He would never do that. Do you remember anything else? What else did he do?"

I gripped my cup with both hands and took another sip of my coffee, already feeling my energy returning. "Nothing else. He left, and I got back to work."

That's odd. Something tugged at my memory as I looked at my left wrist. Slowly I placed my cup down to swipe a finger across my wrist. It was smooth, with blue-colored veins showing beneath my skin.

"What's wrong?" Natalie asked. I looked up at her and then down at my wrist again. Something was wrong here; something was *really wrong*. First, my curtain was drawn at my window; my curtain is always open. And now my scar was gone. A thought occurred to me and I looked over at Natalie once more.

"How did you know where I live?"

She shrugged and puckered her lips. "I went to the admissions office. I told you, I was worried about you."

I didn't believe her.

My eyes widened as she faded, becoming almost transparent right before my eyes, and I got up, almost falling off my stool.

"Who the hell are you?" I reached behind me and grabbed a knife. "Who are you? What do you want from me?"

She tilted her head to the side and dared to look concerned when I was the one looking through her body. "Ruby, you need to calm down."

The wall to my right cracked and I lost it. "Are you fucking kidding me? Tell me who you are right now! What have you done with Natalie? Where is she? What the hell is going on here?"

The knife dropped out of my hand as more walls began to crack and Natalie started to flash in and out of existence. I hadn't taken any drugs, I was sure of it. I've never even done drugs, not even once, so why was I tripping? I must be tripping, because none of this was possible.

My hand fell to my side as I looked into Natalie's eyes. "This isn't real."

I sat up in bed with a start, my breathing shallow as I clutched at my chest. I was under sheets that weren't my own, black silk sheets at that. And when I looked to my left, I backed up so much I almost fell off the bed.

Natalie was sitting in a chair by my bed. No, not my bed. I wasn't even in my room. She was holding her head, her face twisted in pain, with Xavier by her side. His hands were on her shoulders as he begged her to speak to him.

What the hell is going on?

I tried to get out of bed and away from them, but my focus was going in and out, my eyes blurry. Before my very eyes what I was seeing changed from the room with Xavier and Natalie to just Natalie and me in my kitchen.

"What the hell are the two of you doing to me?" My head felt like it was going to explode. There was a weight on my chest so heavy it was like something was sitting on me. "What's going on!?"

Xavier looked my way, his jaw clenched tightly, and Natalie held her hand out to me, her face red. "Sleep."

I wasn't given the chance to fight it. I was hit with a wave of drowsiness that was so strong I was out cold before my head smacked against the cold hard floor.

Ruby

*T*he third time I woke up, I felt like myself. I felt rested, but I was still in a room that wasn't my own. I laid there unmoving, but my sleepy eyes were on the black ceiling. The rest of the room was shrouded in darkness, only illuminated by one lamp that was standing by the door. I waited patiently until I felt truly awake before untangling my hand from the sheet to wipe at the corners of my eyes.

I replayed the events that had led me to be in a bed that wasn't my own and fisted my hands. *How many days have even passed,* I wondered?

I wasn't dead, so that was something, but how long would that last? What had happened in that alleyway hadn't been a dream. Xavier had transformed before my eyes and killed three men. Natalie had created some kind of alternate reality inside my head, and then she magically put me back to sleep after I woke up from it.

I closed my eyes and inhaled deeply before exhaling and then repeated the act once more. I could easily imagine that everything that had happened was impossible, but I would be foolish to do that when I had seen it all with my own eyes. Maybe what had happened with Xavier was a dream.

I rolled onto my side and my heart skipped a beat as I looked into Xavier's eyes. He was sitting in a chair at the far end of the room with one leg crossed over the other. I could only tell it was him when he leaned forward into the light. He was wearing a white T-shirt and washed-out jeans, and even in the light, his face was unreadable as he stared back at me.

He placed his elbows on his knees before interlocking his fingers before him. All I could see as I looked at him was the creature I had seen the previous night, but I was surprised at myself for not feeling fear.

I should be screaming and banging on the door. I should be doing something other than staring at him.

"How are you feeling?"

I sat up and looked down at the white nightgown I was wearing. "You didn't change my clothes, did you?"

"Don't flatter yourself."

"I assure you there is nothing flat on my body except for my stomach."

He combed his hand through his hair, and I watched as

the silky strands jumped back into place. "How are you feeling?" he repeated.

"As good as anyone who's been abducted."

He reclined in the chair, and his face was once again hidden. "Abducted?"

I sighed. I wasn't in the mood to play around with Xavier. I was already calmer than I should be. If he was going to kill me, he would have already, right?

"What happened?"

"You already know. You saw something you shouldn't have."

Well, that confirmed that I wasn't dreaming, and I wished it wasn't so because now I had questions. A lot of them. "I don't remember what I saw."

Maybe if I pretended I hadn't seen anything, he'd let me go. I had a bad feeling about where this conversation was going, and considering that I knew he could rip me to shreds, I shouldn't say anything to upset him. I shouldn't even be thinking certain thoughts. What if he was reading my mind?

He got to his feet and walked over to the bed, his hands buried in his pockets, and my body went stiff. But what really got me was when he stepped into the light and his eyes were as black as they had been that night.

I swallowed hard and threw the covers off me. I stood and looked up at him, into his obsidian eyes, and slapped him across the face.

"You knocked me out."

He reached up and touched his cheek, his head turned to the side. The side of his mouth twitched, and my eyes widened, shocked at what I had just done, but I stood my ground, my legs shaking. If I was going to die, I'd rather die bravely anyway.

"That's what you're worried about?" His head turned back to me. "When you know I could have done so much worse?"

"Are you going to kill me?"

He stepped closer, and my heart started to hammer in my chest. He looked me up and down, as if he was sizing me up, and I clenched my fists so much my nails began to dig into my flesh. Was he checking if he could swallow me whole?

I crossed my arms over my chest and, to my surprise, a smirk found its way onto his lips. It was small, but it was there.

"You're hiding your fear very well, but I can smell it." I lifted my hand again to slap the smug prick, and he caught my wrist. "Hit me again, Ruby, and I will hurt you."

"Where am I? I want to go home, Xavier. I don't care what you are. I'll keep my mouth shut, just let me go home."

He threw my hand down, and I stepped back as I held onto my wrist. He hadn't squeezed me, but if he had so much as a muscle spasm, he would probably shatter the bone in my arm. I had slapped a werewolf. Me, Ruby Saunders.

The black in his eyes disappeared, and he crossed his arms over his chest, causing his shirt to stretch taut over his bulging biceps. I turned away, my eyes scanning the room. "Just let me go."

"I can't do that, and you know it."

I spun on my heels, my temper getting the better of me. "I don't know shit! I don't know shit! I don't even know what you are! What I know is that three men died, and I got knocked out. And now I'm here. And what the hell did you and Natalie do to me? You know what? I don't want to know.

23

I want to forget all of this, and that means you, her, and this entire mess. Now let me go!"

"Any human who learns about werewolves has to die."

My heart stopped beating. I hated how calmly he had just said that. Did I even hear him correctly? I couldn't have.

"What?" I raised a shaky finger to his face as I forced all the bravado I had to the surface. "You've got to be kidding. You're joking, right? How does that make sense, Xavier? That was something you were aware of? And now you're saying something like that so casually, as if you weren't the one who chose to reveal yourself to me?"

We stood in silence for a moment, my angry eyes piercing into his. I watched his face shift from relaxed to furious within seconds. When he took a step toward me, I stepped back, tripped, and fell onto the bed.

"You humans are all the same." His mouth was barely opening as he spoke, but his voice was projecting throughout the room. He was pissed, livid, and my fear pinned me to the bed as he leaned over me. "You humans are all ungrateful. You're ungrateful. I saved you from being raped and murdered, but yes, that was my mistake."

He stood up and stormed from the room and my body jerked as he slammed the door. I swallowed, despite how dry my mouth was, as tears began to roll down my cheeks. I wasn't ungrateful. He had saved me from a horrible attack. But now I was going to be killed by werewolves?

3

XAVIER

*N*ever before have I hated my exceptional hearing until now.

No, that wasn't true. Every day of my life, having to live alongside humans has been a headache. They are loud, messy, and my only place of peace has been my home. Until now.

I rested my elbow on the marble island and pinched the bridge of my nose as Ruby continued to pound on her door on the fourth floor.

Is she going to get tired at any point? She's been at it for an hour.

My hand slid to my cheek as I sat there, still shocked that she had slapped me. She's brave, I'll give her that. Or maybe she isn't as smart as she looks. What human slaps a werewolf when they are fully aware that a werewolf could rip them to shreds?

Images from the night I had killed those men flashed in my mind, and my face morphed into a deep scowl. I took a deep breath, which was what I should have done that night, instead of losing my cool. It was too late now anyway, what was done was done, and now there were consequences to accept.

I didn't feel bad for those men; they got what they deserved. If their victim hadn't been Ruby, it would have been someone else who wouldn't have had someone like me to protect them.

I shook my head. I hadn't actually saved Ruby at all. Because of me, she jumped out of the frying pan and into the fire. By law, werewolf law, she would now have to die. Humans can never be trusted with the truth that the monsters from their Hollywood movies are real. Even though those movies are so inaccurate.

History has proven time and time again that humans can't handle knowing that they are almost at the bottom of the food chain.

"Xavier, fix your face. You look like shit."

I looked over at Natalie as she walked into the kitchen and made a beeline for the fridge.

"She's giving me a headache. She won't stop screaming."

She threw a bottle of water across the room, and I caught it easily as she took a seat at the island. "What do you expect? She just needs time to process things."

"How do you process being told you're going to be killed? Or that werewolves are real?"

She puckered her mouth, looking thoughtful for a moment before shrugging. "You may have a point." She then pointed at me. "She's handling things much better than I expected, though. If I was in her position, I'd die from a heart attack. I think the entire house heard that slap." She chuckled, then sipped her water as I narrowed my eyes. "She's got balls, I'll give her that."

"She's not brave, she's stupid."

Natalie rolled her eyes. "Oh please. Just like how you *should have* walked away and not gotten involved the other night?"

"You know I couldn't," I said through clenched teeth. Her brows furrowed for a moment, and I looked away from the emotions in her eyes. I didn't need her pity for the shit I've landed myself, and ultimately the pack, in with this situation.

Ruby was a problem, a loud fucking problem. It's been years since a human was condemned to death because they've learned of our secret. My father isn't going to be pleased that his son, a pureblood and alpha-to-be for our pack, lost his cool. Now a smart-mouthed human girl who was just in the wrong place at the wrong time would have to die.

My mind took me back to Ruby's room when she had slapped me and made a face. What I should have done was rip her arm off. That's what any other werewolf would have done. I was the son of the alpha, damn it. And here I was, being slapped around by a human as if I was a little pup.

Why didn't I just walk away? I'm a Blackwood. I should have fought my urges and kept moving because a smart wolf would have seen past his anger and known that once she saw the truth she'd have to die anyway.

But her screams had been deafening, her fear so thick that the scent was overpowering.

A loud crash echoed through the house, and I winced as I clenched my fists. She was going to draw more attention to herself. Only a handful of people knew about her presence on the pack grounds, and it needed to remain that way, for now anyway.

I combed my hair back, my ears twitching now that she finally had stopped screaming for help. "You know this is a delicate situation, Natalie." Her eyes grew serious and I crossed my arms on the island as I leaned forward, "No one can know what's really going on here. What's really going on with…"

"Thank Jesus, she finally stopped screaming." I swallowed my words as Anna walked into the kitchen, her brown hair up in its usual high ponytail. "Someone needs to kill that human bitch already. Why is she here and not in one of the cells? I knew she looked like trouble from the day I saw her at that diner."

My fist came down hard on the counter as I growled. Anna gasped and drew back, her eyes wide with shock. I pinned her with a stare that had her scurrying out of the kitchen, and it only annoyed me further when Natalie started laughing.

"I think that's the first time I've seen you get upset at Anna. She's like an itch under your feet when you're wearing sneakers. She seriously needs to get over her obsession with you."

"Natalie, be nice."

She snorted. "Oh, like you just were? I still don't know how you managed to date her for a year."

Natalie and I looked to the door as my father walked in. Just like that, the headache that had finally eased returned with a vengeance.

"Natalie, what did you find out?"

"Alpha Mathieu, you're back. Um, I'm sorry, but I did not

learn much. She saw through the illusion I created in her mind. I wasn't able to get anything from her, but I can tell you she's not a threat." Natalie bit down on her lip. "There's some kind of block in her mind. It's like a wall, but a strong one. I couldn't get through. The more I pushed the more painful it was for me."

Mathieu Blackwood, alpha to the Blackmoon Pack and my father, had a look on his face that I didn't like. This was a problem our pack did not need, especially right now. At forty-eight years old, he didn't look a day over thirty. He's six foot seven with a thick black beard and black eyes, just like mine. Just looking at him was intimidating, never mind the intensity that seemed to roll off him in waves. There was a time when I had feared him just like everyone else does, but not anymore. I'm to take his place soon. A strong alpha fears no one.

"Xavier." I looked up from the salt shaker that had been holding my attention. I knew what was coming. "This shouldn't have happened. You, out of all the wolves here, should not have lost control like that. And for a human! Alphas *must* have control, Xavier. Explain yourself."

Natalie's brows touched her hairline as she made a sound in the back of her throat. I threw her a look, and so did Mathieu. "What is it, Natalie?"

"You're not going to like what he has to say." She bowed to my father with respect before glancing up at him from under her lashes. "With all due respect, Alpha, Xavier didn't have a choice in the matter. They were going to rape her."

Mathieu frowned as his dark eyes darted from Natalie to me and then back. "So, what is it then? Someone needs to explain exactly what happened before this has to be reported to the Council. They won't give a shit about a human girl being raped."

"That's because the Council is made up of sick old bastards who only care about themselves."

Mathieu exhaled heavily with exasperation. "Natalie!"

"Sorry."

"The Council is there to protect us. You two might not have been around back when we were at war before, but another war, in this day and age, would lead to our extinction. We stay hidden in order to stay alive." He looked my way. "So all humans who find out about us *have* to die."

Over my dead body was Ruby going to die for my fuckup. This wasn't her fault.

"We'll have to talk in your office, Dad."

He frowned.

Living with wolves means privacy is limited because everyone has supernatural hearing. He knew that suggesting we talk in his office, which was soundproof, meant something was wrong.

He nodded and walked away. Natalie folded her lips inward, an apologetic look on her face, as I followed my father to the fourth floor.

I was about to pull the pin from a grenade by explaining to Dad why I had saved Ruby.

Natalie

I balanced the tray in my left hand as I knocked and opened Ruby's door. I frowned at the shattered lamp by the door before poking my head inside.

"Ruby? It's Natalie." I closed the door behind me when I found her sitting on the floor at the back of the room, her head against the wall. "I brought something for you to eat. You must be hungry."

She opened her eyes slowly, her cold stare making me rethink approaching her. I placed the tray on the coffee table before the sofa and sighed. Her eyes and nose were red from crying and her hair was wild and tangled. She looked a mess, and my heart went out to her. The hatred in her eyes cut me deeply, but I deserved it as much as Xavier.

She had witnessed three men being ripped to shreds, and now she was locked away in a room awaiting her own death. I'd want to rip some fucking limbs off myself if I was her.

Sighing, I pulled a chair closer to her but stayed at a polite distance so she wouldn't feel crowded. "I know you must be confused right now, and scared. I'll answer any questions you have."

Ruby only stared at me, her eyes dull and emotionless. This change was odd considering she had been screaming at the top of her voice less than an hour ago. The brave girl I had heard slap Xavier now looked broken and defeated, or was she just tired from screaming?

She looked toward the window at the swaying trees outside. I did the same thing, allowing her to speak on her own terms. I wasn't confident she would speak at all. Maybe our approach had been the wrong one, trying to pry into her

31

mind instead of speaking to her. She had witnessed something previously unimaginable to her, and then I went in and stirred up her brain with my power. Too much was happening to her with little to no explanation or preparation.

Xavier certainly hadn't made the situation better by telling her she was going to be killed.

"What were you doing to me?" I looked in her direction, but she was still staring out the window. She looked so broken, so confused. "You were inside my head."

"I'm sorry, my alpha ordered me to." She finally looked my way and I sighed. "Okay. Some of the things you've seen in the movies about werewolves are true, and some are bullshit. We do live in packs. We do have an alpha. However, we don't change only during the full moon, and silver doesn't hurt us. We don't communicate telepathically, and we don't look the way you'd expect."

Ruby released the knees she had been holding to her chest and stretched her legs out. I took that as a sign of her slowly relaxing and starting to process what had happened.

"I'm not like Xavier and the others, though. I'm an Enchanted, a female wolf (or she-wolf if you will) who cannot and will never be able to transform. I still have exceptional hearing, speed, sight, and strength, but nothing compared to, say, Xavier. However, I have different powers of my own that no one else in the pack shares. All packs have an Enchanted, some more powerful than others. That's how I was inside your mind. I wasn't trying to hurt you, Ruby. I was trying to see if you're a threat to my people."

She scoffed at that and looked away. "I'm in a house filled with werewolves, and I'm the threat?"

I smiled; she had a point. "That's true, but humans are powerful in their own way. Humans are a danger to the supernatural world. That's why all supernatural creatures have their own way of dealing with humans who learn of their existence."

"What others are there? You said all supernatural creatures."

She was curious, and I was happy to tell her anything she wanted to know. At least it took her mind off the inevitable. Seeing auras was one of my gifts, and I had been drawn to hers from the moment I saw her. Pure white auras like Ruby's were rare. Very rare.

"There are witches, golems, demons, angels, gods, the whole works. They're all real. Some live alongside humans just like us wolves, and some live in other dimensions."

"When?"

I frowned. "When what?"

"When are *your people* going to kill me?"

I inhaled deeply. Even though I expected the question, it still caught me off guard. She didn't look sad or upset, she looked defeated. Somehow that was worse. "I don't know." She released a breath she seemed to have been holding in, and I could hear her heart rate spike. "Listen, Xavier is doing what he can right now to save you, okay?"

She arched a brow. "Xavier? He's trying to save me?" She laughed, but it held no humor. I frowned, not sure what she was laughing at. Was she losing her mind? "Xavier trying to save me is exactly what got me into this mess. Honestly, I don't like him, and it's clear he doesn't like me either." She leaned forward. "Let me go, please. I won't tell anyone. Use your powers and wipe my memory if you must. Why can't you do that?"

"I wish it was that easy." I got up and walked toward her, but her body tensed and her heartbeat increased to a frantic pace. She was scared of me. "You don't have to be scared of me, Ruby."

She got to her feet shakily and I listened as her stomach growled. She braced herself on the wall for a moment, then pushed forward and approached me. Her aura turned so white it was almost blinding, forcing me to avoid looking directly at her.

Where her eyes had been dull a moment ago, they now filled with a mix of anger and sadness. She stopped just before me. "I don't want to die."

"You're not going to. Listen to me Ruby, take it easy on Xavier. This has never happened before. It's new to him."

She threw her hands in the air, her brows knitting as she grew frustrated. She turned away, pacing to the window and then back toward me. "And I'm new to being abducted! I'm new to this, new to all of this! What exactly is new to him, Natalie? What? Help me to understand what he's used to, because I'm the one trapped inside this room waiting to find out if I'm going to live to see another day."

Silence fell between us. Our conversation wasn't going the way I had wanted it to, and I realized I had been foolish to think it would be any different. At this point, the less she knew the better. I couldn't explain to her why she could never be harmed in our pack. That was Xavier's story to tell.

She walked over to the bed and sat down, but I remained standing. Only a few days ago I had thought I had made a friend, the first human I'd ever found myself drawn to. It would have been best if I had kept my distance. The moment I sat down beside her at that table in the library, I had set the wheels of this disaster in motion.

This wasn't Xavier's fault. It was mine.

She tilted her head. "If it's your law to kill all humans who learn about your existence, then why try and save me?"

Shit.

Seeing the look on my face, she shook her head. "Forget it."

"You'll get explanations soon enough. You just have to trust me, okay?"

She arched a brow. "Trust you? *Trust you?* I don't know what to make of any of this. I'm still trying to figure out if this is all some sick prank. Werewolves and supernaturals are real, and I'm going to die because I know about it? I can't believe any of it. Trust is a two-way street, Natalie. Just leave me alone, okay?"

I understood her irritation, but I was only trying to be her friend. I'm still a wolf, with a temper just like any other wolf, and she was starting to piss me off.

"Fine. You're not going to die, Ruby, but I can't guarantee you'll ever be able to leave this pack. A human hasn't knowingly come into contact with a werewolf in a long time, and never from our pack. There's so much you don't know. If you want to live, I suggest when the alpha comes to see you, you should try to be chill and not snappy. Your emotions are all over the place, and understandably so, but it's certainly not in your best interest to piss him off."

I turned and left, leaving her as she had asked me to. No matter how annoyed I was, I knew her attitude and anger were warranted.

As an Enchanted, I'm allowed to be around humans more than Xavier or any other wolf. As long as I have control over my powers, that is. Even so, I'd never been interested in having a human friend until I met Ruby. Although, in truth, I mistook her for a supernatural until I smelled her. Her incredible aura had tricked me into thinking she was supernatural that day in the library. I had wanted to find out which type, but she just smelled human. Her personality had done the rest. I didn't want any harm to come to her. I really didn't want to lose my friend.

I came to a stop at the stairs and watched Xavier remove his shirt and jump off one of the balconies.

4

RUBY

*Y*ou're *not going to die, Ruby, but I can't guarantee you'll ever be able to leave this pack.*

Natalie's words ran through my mind in an endless loop. With each refrain, I felt another piece of my life crack up and slowly disintegrate. What had she meant? I can't stay here with a bunch of werewolves! Where even is "here"?

She had come to me to shed some light on my situation, and I had given her the cold shoulder. It was killing me. She didn't have to come to see me. She didn't have to offer any explanation, but she had. She'd even brought food for me, and I still pushed her away, the only friend I might have here.

But she's still one of them. It makes no difference that she's an "Enchanted" or whatever she called herself. She's still one of them. If Xavier's attempt to spare my life doesn't work, she'll have to stand by and watch me be killed.

Xavier Blackwood.

I rolled onto my back as that name echoed in my mind. I definitely thought he was strange, even before I learned he has fangs. Now, thanks to him, I'm not even sure whether I'm going to live or die. It's because of him I'm in this mess, but there's something about him that keeps pulling my thoughts back to him.

From the moment I'd seen him in that library, I had gotten the sense that he wasn't really happy. It seemed like he was just going through the motions in life and trying to make the best of it, kind of like I was.

I held my hand up and over my face before curling my fingers into a fist and resting it against my chest. I had looked into the eyes of a monster and had felt no fear. I had slapped him. Hard. I still couldn't believe I'd done it. Why was he trying to save me? It was obvious he didn't like me, so why go out of his way to save me to begin with, especially knowing I'd then have to be killed? Why go against your own law to spare a human's life, my life?

Was it guilt?

I had too many questions, and no one to ask for answers. Werewolves, witches, gods...they're all real. All the things that go bump in the night are real, and now I'm a part of that world. Or I will be for however long I'm permitted to live anyway. No, I don't want this. I rolled onto my other side to face the window and yawned, having not slept a wink the night before. Outside the moon's light was exceptionally bright, causing the trees to cast their shadows inside my room.

I could hear the wind howling outside...or was that a wolf?

I closed my eyes, all out of tears to shed, and fell into a deep sleep.

Do you prefer to die than to live? I woke up with a start to those words in my head.

The voice inside my head had asked a good question. I looked around the room and realized it was morning. It felt like I had only just closed my eyes to sleep.

However, being trapped here as a prisoner forever among people who hate my species isn't what I call living. Dying didn't sound fun, either. I should be thinking of ways to escape, but I'd be a moron to think I could get out without a house full of werewolves noticing. There was no way I could outrun a werewolf, let alone a pack of them.

Time to face facts: life as I knew it was over.

Two days. I enjoyed life at college for two whole days before this shit show began. I'd long since lost track of time. I was not sure how many days had passed since I was brought here, but I knew I could kiss that scholarship goodbye.

I shook my head and turned my back to the window. There was only one explanation – I was cursed. I think I've always known. It's time to stop pretending. What are the odds of almost being raped, only to be saved by a werewolf, who then tells you it's their law to kill any human who sees them?

Am I the only one who sees how ridiculous this is? I'm at risk of being killed for being saved. If cursed doesn't explain it, I don't know what does.

Unable to lie in bed any longer, I got up and took a quick shower. Thank God there was a bathroom and a room with a bed at least. I'd thought they'd throw humans into dark dank cells. I pulled on the jeans and top that I had woken up to find on the sofa across the room. There was a comb, tooth-brush, deodorant, and other necessities in the bathroom as well. In addition to being given all these things to be comfortable, I was being fed twice a day. It seemed I would escape the "immediate death" option.

A quick glance in the mirror showed me I was starting to look pale from being inside for so long. If I'm forced to deal with another week or even a month of this, I'll become practically transparent. I couldn't help noticing how good my skin looked otherwise, though. There seemed to be a glow to my skin and a brightness to my eyes that had never been there before. I also felt a strength within my muscles that I'd never felt before. Maybe it was all the sleep I was getting?

I shook my head and threw the hairbrush down in disgust. I wasn't at a spa retreat, for God's sake. I was trapped in a house filled with monsters.

Do they hunt and eat people? How long will I survive living here before someone decides I look like a tasty snack?

I was making my way across the room to sit by the window when a knock came at the door, and it opened. My body grew tense and my heart pounded like a drum in my ears as the largest man I'd ever seen in my life walked into the room.

His body almost filled the doorway, and I swallowed hard as he bent his head to walk under the door frame.

He was tall, six foot seven, maybe? His eyes were black pools, and his beard was thick. It took me only a moment to realize he must be Mathieu Blackwood, Xavier's father and alpha of this pack. When I first heard Natalie mention him, I might have looked him up online. Just out of curiosity, of course. I hadn't been able to find any pictures of him, despite him being a millionaire.

Were all wolves this large?

He looked me up and down, his eyes and face revealing nothing of what he might be thinking. Like the good human I am, one who doesn't want to be eaten, I stayed quiet and rooted in place.

"Come."

He turned and walked away, leaving the door open for me to follow him. He didn't spare a glance behind him to make sure I was following. He knew I wasn't going to defy him.

I walked behind him quietly, my eyes trying to absorb as much of my surroundings as possible. I had imagined the house to be dark and mysterious, semi-lit, with antique furniture and creepy halls. As we descended a large double staircase, and then another and another before going outside, I was pleasantly surprised at how beautiful the house was. The décor was simple but elegant, with gold-handled doors and marble floors. Mathieu Blackwood wasn't just a were-wolf; he was a wealthy man. Why would he not be living comfortably?

Yes, I'm curious about him, as well as Xavier and Natalie. I want to know what they are, what it means to be what they are. I want to know their history and their plans for their future. If I'm now linked to these people, I want to know everything about them. And not just werewolves for that matter.

I've always been a fan of the supernatural, and now I was a prisoner in their world. I might as well gain a better under-standing of my new reality.

Once we were outside, I paused to stare up at the house, my hand on my forehead to shield my eyes from the morning sun.

I closed my eyes for a moment as I inhaled the scent of

41

fresh air, and with my head tilted up to the sky, I smiled as I felt the sun warming my skin. My body relaxed for the first time in days as I felt the cool breeze brush over me. The view from my room had shown nothing but trees upon trees, so I had known we were in the woods. But actually being outside, smelling the fresh air, was so soothing.

"When I was younger, I used to do the same."

Just like that, my euphoric haze crashed back into reality. Since I had stopped walking and had fallen behind, distracted by the world around me, I hadn't realized he had returned to my side. Mathieu's deep baritone voice caused the air to vibrate with each word he spoke, pulling me from my daydream.

"I'd stand and inhale the air. The air in the city is stuffy, tainted." He looked down at me, and although he wasn't smiling, he wasn't looking at me with hatred either. "Do you like the house?"

Was this man really asking me about his house right now?

"I do. It's not what I was expecting."

He scoffed at that. "I know." He looked up at the house. "This house has been in my family for generations, with a few renovations here and there, of course. This is my home and the home for many wolves." He looked down at me. "A human being here puts them all, us all, in great jeopardy."

I swallowed. "Sir, I find it hard to open a jar of jam sometimes. I'm no danger to any werewolf, let alone a pack of them."

His brow arched. "Are you scared?"

"I'm scared of being killed. I don't want to die."

"Are you scared of the monsters that are surrounding you right now?"

42

I looked back as a man walked through the door we had just exited. He was shirtless, with both his arms covered in tattoos. I watched as he paused, sniffed the air, and then looked my way.

He stood there, his eyes piercing mine before he suddenly took off at a run. My eyes widened as within seconds he disappeared into the woods. Though my heart was hammering in my chest, I realized it wasn't from fear but excitement, and from curiosity about how he was able to do that. No, I wasn't scared of werewolves. They were people, just not the kind I was used to. It's not like I have a great love for humans anyway. Most people annoy me to no end.

"I'm not scared of werewolves unless one decides to attack me. What I am is curious. I want to know more. Humans, I know all about, and sometimes I wish I didn't. Werewolves are all new."

After a few seconds had passed without a response from Mathieu, I looked his way and found him staring down at me.

Shit, had I said something wrong?

"I um…"

"I'll release you," he said as he cut me off, and my mouth dropped open. "I'll release you to attend school and to work. I understand you work at a diner in the city. But you will be living here from now on. You may come and go as you please, but you will remain under my watch, my care. Say nothing about what we are to anyone, and I'll have no reason to harm you."

His threat didn't go unnoticed by me. I wasn't being given freedom exactly, I was just getting a long leash. My mouth opened and closed, and he tilted his head to the side as he watched me. I didn't have to ask. I knew my options were to take this deal or die.

"Okay," I replied, my voice a mere whisper. "But why? It's your law to kill any human who finds out about werewolves. It's already clear to me that humans are hated, that I'm hated. Why spare me and invite me to live with you?"

He turned his back to the house as he buried his hands in his pockets, his crisp white shirt stretching somewhat. We stood in silence, both of us listening to the sounds of the forest, but I knew he was hearing so much more than I was.

"My son spoke to me, as did Natalie. They've both convinced me to let you stay. There will be a time when humans and werewolves will have to come together again. And if you tell anyone I said that I'll rip your throat out." My eyes widened but I kept my eyes forward. "Times are changing, and we need to change with them. My wolves need to be comfortable around a human. We'll learn from you, and you'll learn from us. That seems fair, doesn't it?"

"Yes."

In my peripheral vision, I saw him nod his head and remove his large hands from his pockets. I was all too aware that those would be the hands to strangle me if I ever stepped out of line. Would the alpha do such a messy job, or would he get some sort of enforcer to do the deed? Would it be Xavier?

"The human saying is, 'keep your friends close and your enemies closer'." He looked down at me. In my mind, I heard jail cells slamming closed. "You will be moved to a different room, and someone will bring your things from your apartment. I'm afraid I must go, but it was nice talking to you, Ruby. I see what Natalie saw in you."

Ruby

nother sleepless night had me restless, my thoughts keeping me awake despite my tired eyes.

My new room would be ready tomorrow, the start of a new life as a guinea pig to werewolves. Mathieu had said his wolves would learn from me, but what was I supposed to teach them? Don't they all live alongside humans anyway? What had he meant when he said one day humans and werewolves would have to come together? He had also said *again*. Did that mean humans used to live alongside werewolves?

"I see what Natalie saw in you."

What had she seen? I still couldn't believe she had taken a deep dive into my mind. Maybe if I hadn't told her to leave me alone, I could've found her and asked her to put me to sleep the way she had before. In the daytime, I can force myself to think of other things, but night causes my doubts and fears to come alive and plague me.

I wasn't even sure if I was handling this all correctly. What's the correct way to deal with something like this anyways? First I'm to be killed, and now I'm a part of the family? Something else was going on here.

"Too many questions," I groaned as I pressed my thumbs against my temples.

Well, if I couldn't sleep, I might as well try to find something to eat. Since this was now my new home, I doubted

anyone would hurt me if I took a walk to the kitchen, wher-
ever that was.

It's easy to get an anxiety attack when you know you're
sneaking around a house that's filled with people who can
hear a pin drop from a mile away. The house was deathly
quiet as I made my way to the first floor. I'd left my slippers
in my room, figuring I'd be quieter in my bare feet, but it
probably didn't matter. They'd hear me anyway.

I reached the first floor and heard a noise. I decided to
check it out. Hopefully, whoever else was wandering around
the house would be friendly enough to point me in the direction of the kitchen. I hadn't eaten anything all day, my
appetite having been wiped away by the bomb Mathieu had
dropped.

"Bingo!" I said under my breath as I spotted the kitchen.
But as I entered it, I found Natalie staring right at me.

"You heard me coming?"

She smiled shyly and nodded. "Are you hungry?"

I nodded as well and walked further into the kitchen. My
brow rose at her neon pink night set. "Yeah, I have a
headache."

She got up from the island and walked over to the fridge.
"So, I guess Mathieu spoke to you, then. It's not so bad here,
once you get used to it."

She pulled out some rotisserie chicken and shoved it into
the microwave before pouring us both some orange juice. I
narrowed my eyes at her as she took her seat once more, the
microwave rumbling behind her. She didn't seem upset with
me, though not exactly her perky self either.

"I'm sorry for how I behaved before," I said.

She smiled again, although this time wider. "It's okay. I can't even imagine how confused and upset you've been."

I made a face as I took a sip of the juice, my eyes taking in everything in the kitchen. "Oh no, this has all been so much fun."

She chuckled, catching on to my sarcasm, and I smiled back, feeling like we were back where we were a few days ago. Before I had been attacked by disgusting men and kidnapped by a pissed-off wolf.

"I want to know more," I told her as she grabbed the chicken and split it in half. "About you, all of you. Why do you all hate humans so much that if one finds out about your existence, you kill them?"

Her hand paused in handing me my plate and a shadow flashed over her blue eyes for a moment. I took the plate from her, and she retreated to her side of the island.

"It's not that we hate humans." She puckered her lips. "Well, some wolves do, but I don't. Wolves and humans just have a bad history, a history that led to a lot of deaths on both sides." She inhaled after swallowing a piece of her chicken. "Decades upon decades ago humans and wolves lived together in peace, along with witches and other supernatural beings. Now those times were as dangerous as you might imagine because there's good and bad in all species. I don't remember the whole story, so I'll summarize what I remember; I haven't heard it since I was a child."

I nodded as I washed my chicken down and folded my arms on the cold marble island. From the look on her face, I could tell I wasn't going to like this story. Since wolves now hate humans and humans don't know of their existence, something horrible must have happened.

She looked broken, however, and I had a feeling she remembered the story a lot better than she was letting on.

"Werewolves aren't predators. We've always been protectors. We have the strength to hunt other supernatural creatures that plague the world. So back then there was a wolf pack living close to a human city. Both species found a balance. The wolves guarded the city and protected the humans, the king's castle, and their own pack as well. Things got complicated when a human girl fell for a wolf. However, there was a human boy who liked her as well." Natalie swiped her tongue across her top lip. "The human boy could not accept that a wolf had 'stolen' his girl, but obviously a human can't fight a wolf. The fight is lost before it even begins."

"The human boy did something stupid, didn't he? I feel like that's where this story is going. This stuff is always about love and jealousy."

She pointed her fork at me. "Listen. Eventually, the wolf found his mate and his relationship with the human girl ended. She was devastated and angry, so she ran right into the arms of the human boy who had loved her all along. On her wedding day, she and her new husband invited her old love, and they arranged for the wolf to be poisoned."

My eyes widened. "What?" After a few seconds of her saying nothing else, I leaned forward. "And what happened after that?"

"That's it. The human girl was the king's daughter, and the wolf was the alpha's son. You can imagine how that all played out, and here we are now, divided. Wolves turned themselves into myths to keep away from humans."

I sat back and sighed. "I can definitely agree that the

princess was a total bitch for doing that. I can even understand why you all retreated to the shadows. But why release
me, yet keep me here? I'm not going to tell anyone, and who
would believe me?"

She ate another piece of chicken and waved the bone at
me. "Someone will, trust me. That's all it'll take to start
another war. Humans are more dangerous now than they
were back then. Humans from this century are even more
jealous, greedy, and power-hungry than before. And on top
of that, now there are bombs, guns, and scientists that
would..."

She trailed off, her anger was bubbling to the surface and
her face twisting, and I couldn't say I didn't understand why.
It's never been difficult for me to put myself in another's
shoes, and right now I could see the pain in Natalie's eyes.
No one wants to imagine themselves cut open on a cold table
while doctors run experiments on them.

"You're right," I replied softly, and she looked over at me.
"A war now would be bad, but why can't I just…"

"Give it a rest, Ruby." Natalie and I watched as Xavier
walked over to the fridge and removed a bottle of water. I
hadn't seen him since the day I had slapped him, and my fist
tightened around my glass as he pinned me with a stare that
could freeze water. I sent one back his way.

"Give it a rest? Are you serious? I'm being forced to stay
here, with people who hate me just because I don't have
fangs. Send someone to tail me, since you don't trust me not
to talk. You've ruined my life, Xavier. I don't belong here!"

He slammed the bottled water down onto the counter
and I jumped. Even Natalie flinched as the bottle burst. "I've
ruined your life? You're so selfish and self-centered. Even

49

after hearing what Natalie had just told you, you still really don't get it? You don't want to be here, but there are people here who don't want you here either. Our pack doesn't kill humans. We've never had to. So you can't leave here, ever. You're lucky your life was even spared, but now I realize I should have left you in that alleyway to be raped!"

"Xavier, that's enough!" Natalie yelled, but it was too late.

"No," I said softly as I got up from the island. "He's right."

Natalie stood up as well. "Ruby, he didn't…"

"I'm going to bed. Goodnight."

I turned away and left the kitchen quickly before either of them could see the tear that fell from my eye.

5

RUBY

I stared at my laptop screen, but I wasn't seeing the coursework I had to do. It had been a week since I'd been sentenced to my new life, but instead of physically going to school I decided to take online classes. I still had my job at the diner, but morning shifts only.

Taking online classes meant I'd have to leave my room less, and I figured that would be best for everyone. I'd now settled into the routine of waiting until everyone's turned in for the night before making myself dinner.

I was accustomed to being alone, but living under these circumstances had me slowly losing my mind. How much of this would I have to endure? Weeks? Months?

Years?

I closed my laptop screen and reclined in the chair by my window as the sun began to set. The splash of colors above the green trees looked like picture-perfect computer wallpaper, and this has been my spot to sit and relax over the last couple of days.

Saying my new room was large was an understatement. I

had my own living room, for crying out loud. And a bath-room that was larger than my old apartment. I hated to say it, but I was living comfortably for the most part, other than the isolation.

I hadn't seen Natalie or Xavier since our chat in the kitchen, and I didn't want to see either of them. Sure, Natalie hadn't done anything, but I wasn't sure I'd be able to handle the pity in her eyes. As for Xavier, I wouldn't mind never seeing him again.

Ever!

With leaving for work early in the morning and getting breakfast at the diner, I'd only run into a few wolves at a distance. However, the looks that I'd gotten would make anyone want to dig a hole and crawl into it. Getting home in the evening after work was even more daunting since there were even more evil stares and whispers to endure.

I got up and stripped, ready to take my shower before bed. I wasn't hungry tonight. My appetite disappeared after I got home and ran into two female wolves standing by the door. I hadn't been scared when one of them flashed her fangs. I didn't even flinch, which impressed even me. But you can only take so much hatred being aimed at you every day.

I stood under the warm water and allowed it to roll down my body. I switched the shower off and roughly dried my hair with a towel.

The only good I was seeing in this situation so far was that I didn't have to pay for rent or food. All I have to do is take my classes and go to work. So many people would kill for this, but would they be able to handle the price that comes with it?

The moment my head touched my pillow, Xavier's face

appeared within my mind. His hurtful words to me began to ring in my ears. I've never felt so ashamed, hurt, and humiliated in all my life. There isn't any love lost between Xavier and me. I can't stand being around the guy without feeling nauseous, and it has nothing to do with his good looks. Yes, I have invaded his home, but to say something like that just wasn't right.

I rolled onto my back, my arms spread wide on my king-sized bed, annoyed at myself because I could see how I'd come off as ungrateful. But my life has changed so much in such a short time! I've been given a lot to process and a lot to accept. I was given the choice to pick death or the only other available option. That wasn't a choice in my eyes.

I was studying law, so the significance wasn't lost on me that Mathieu was breaking werewolf law by keeping me alive and a secret. Now when, not if, my existence is discovered, what will happen to me? What will happen to him and his pack?

I can see it now – I'll be blamed for that as well.

"I should have left you in that alleyway to be raped!"

I rolled onto my side and pulled the sheet up to my chin, a stinging within my eyes forcing me to squeeze them shut as tears began to soak my pillow.

I'm not ungrateful. What I am is trapped and dying slowly.

Ruby

A nearby sound penetrated my sleep, but only enough for an eye to crack open and then immediately close again. I was exhausted after spending hours crying.

It was the first time I've cried, a true cry, since the start of the downward spiral my life has taken. There is a time for everyone when a cry that's started by one thing becomes a cry about everything, things from your past and present. You let all your emotions out and leave yourself bare, but afterward, you feel so numb, so light, the only thing left to do is sleep, a dead sleep.

The next time the sound came, however, it was enough to wake me completely. I sat straight up, my eyes darting around my room frantically.

Why did that howl sound so loud? So close?

I gripped the sheets at my sides as I listened. The night had returned to silence, but shortly after, another howl rang out. A horrible feeling settled in the pit of my stomach. Throughout my time here I hadn't seen a single wolf in wolf form. I hadn't even heard so much as a growl until now.

I had been expecting to see shirtless men walking around, and multiple brawls, or at least being forced to buy earplugs to drown out the howling at night. In reality, I've never slept so well in my entire life. Whenever my thoughts allowed me to fall asleep, that is.

Another howl penetrated the walls, but this one wasn't as loud. It sounded more like a wounded animal, and I swung my legs over the side of my bed and got up.

Yes, going snooping right now was a bad idea, but was I still going to do it?

Damn skippy.

I peeped out my door and looked up and down the corridor before slipping out and closing my door as softly as possible. Outside my room, I could now hear more howls. Quieter ones, but they were there. The further I walked from my room, the louder they got, but I was certain they were coming from outside.

No, I wasn't going to go outside. I'm not that stupid. But I was peering through every window I passed to see if I could catch a glimpse of anything outside.

Maybe a party is going on, I thought to myself. But with each window I passed, I saw nothing. If a party was going on, I'd hear music. I'd see people.

I paused and puckered my lips. Why do I never see more than ten people around, including Natalie and Xavier? There must be others. So are there other houses within the woods that I haven't seen? It would make sense if that was the case since this was the alpha's house. It should be separate from the pack, the community.

My brow arched as I realized there might be an entire little town here in the forest.

A piercing howl cut through my thoughts, and my steps faltered. The sound reverberated into the house through a window just up ahead. I walked over slowly, my heart in my throat, wondering what I'd see. Oh boy, was I not prepared!

Forget what you've seen in the movies of men turning into actual wolves on four legs. It's bullshit.

In the backyard were two wolves… creatures… beasts… restraining a man with chains. And Xavier was there, too. I couldn't hear what was being said – they were too far away – but my eyes were glued to the two beasts.

There were tiki torches all around them, as if a ritual was being held, the flames from the fires at their tips illuminating the darkness. The wolves were standing on two legs, their bodies covered in thick fur, their mouths no longer mouths but snouts, although shorter than a normal wolf. Their ears were large, long, and pointy, but I was surprised at how much their physique still looked human. Their abs and bulging muscles were still visible through their smooth fur. They looked to be at least seven feet tall, maybe more, with their backs slightly hunched. As I watched, their long tails agitatedly swiped back and forth.

Jesus, they're really real.

I swallowed the lump that had formed in my throat and moved to the side of the window, peeking around the frame. The last thing I wanted was to be caught snooping on something that was clearly private.

Was that man before Xavier human?

My eyes drifted back to the wolves as a sudden urge to be close to them, to touch their fur and feel the strength in their arms, overtook me. Yes, they were scary, but they were truly majestic beings as well. One of them shifted his weight from one leg to the other and the clear power as his muscles rippled had a smile forming on my lips. I bit down on my nail. I felt like I was going into shock the longer I stared at them. My breath caught as the man in chains lashed out at Xavier. Odd that my heart would skip a beat for Xavier's safety, but he didn't even flinch. I couldn't see his face clearly, just his profile cloaked in shadows.

I couldn't tell if he was speaking, but the man in chains was becoming more furious, pulling and twisting until he fell to the ground. The wolves quickly yanked him back to his feet. Suddenly, a tail swiped at Xavier, the tail belonging to the man in chains. I guess he was a wolf after all, though he wasn't fully transformed. Xavier leaned back and avoided the blow, and my hand flew to my mouth as I gasped at what happened next. Xavier reached forward, and his entire hand vanished inside the man's chest.

My body started shaking as he stepped toward the man and then yanked his hand out. I gagged, and although I wanted to step away from the window, I couldn't look away as he dropped the heart that was in his hand while the wolves caught the lifeless body.

What did I just watch?

My heart was pounding so loud it was drowning out the growls from the wolves. I'd just watched Xavier take a life! I was in shock, no doubt, but what had I just watched? That man was a wolf, one of his kind, so why kill him like that?

The two wolves walked away with the body and Xavier watched them leave. Then his head lifted as if smelling the air. Before I could step away from the window, his eyes pierced into mine. The next thing I knew, my legs were taking me back to my room as if I was being chased.

Ruby

*F*alling asleep again had been hard. I had lain in bed on my back with my sheets up to my chin, but my eyes were trained on my door, wondering if at any moment Xavier would burst in to confront me for snooping around last night. I had seen something I shouldn't have, that was very clear.

My brain kept replaying him reaching into that man's chest as easily as if it was butter and his hand was a knife. He had seemed indifferent, almost as if he was doing a mundane task like buttering his bread, not taking a life.

I realized that while I'd been so busy isolating myself, I'd also been wasting the chance I'd been given to learn about the people I'd be spending an unknown amount of time with. Hiding away in my room was not the way to survive in this new life.

I rolled onto my side and scratched at my cheek as the morning sun began to warm my skin. I was thankful to have a window close to my bed, to be able to wake up to the feel of the sun. Much as I wasn't into the mood to get out of bed, I decided it was time to get out of this room and explore the house I was living in. Natalie seemed to be the only person willing to talk to me, so I'd start by hunting her down and getting answers to all my questions.

I opened my eyes and had to bite down on my lip to stop the scream from escaping. Xavier's black eyes calmly watched as I rolled to the other side of my bed and away from him.

"What the hell are you doing here?" I asked as I pulled the sheet up to cover my chest. How long had he been sitting by my bed and watching me sleep?

"Are you scared of me?"

I frowned. My irritation began to fade as I took in his appearance. He was wearing a black T-shirt and sat with his arms crossed over his broad chest, his massive size making me wonder if the chair would collapse.

He arched a brow and I looked away, blinking rapidly to rid myself of the image of him killing that man. The man sitting beside my bed didn't look like a killer.

"He had lost his mate," he said, and I looked over at him. "All werewolves have a mate, a partner. At their first meeting, they instinctively know they're meant for each other. The legends say the bond ensures each wolf meets another who complements them perfectly in order to strengthen their bloodlines. Not all mates end up together, however. But a wolf rejecting another is rare." His jaw clenched tightly and he looked away. "When you meet your mate, it feels like a part of your life that you didn't know was broken off glues itself back together." He inhaled and unfolded his arms, both hands combing his hair back. The side of his mouth arched. "So when you lose that person, the pain is unbearable."

He pinned me with his eyes, and I couldn't look away. Why did he look so broken?

"He was a good man, but after losing his mate he made several attempts to take his own life."

My eyes widened as my brows knit tightly and my mouth turned downward. I've never been in love before, but to love someone so much that if they die, you wish to be dead as well seemed unreal to me. I looked away as my feelings of horror from watching that man die turned into pity. I remembered the way he had been lashing out at Xavier, the way he had been crying. And to know it was all because he had lost his mate made the situation so much worse. Xavier hadn't murdered another person; he had saved a person from unimaginable emotional pain.

"Instead of allowing him to die like that, I gave him an honorable death." He leaned forward and I glanced at him from the corner of my eye. "So, do you think we're monsters? That I'm a monster?"

"No." The word had escaped my mouth too quickly. "I mean, having seen what you guys really look like, you don't look like angels but, no, you're not monsters. You've explained what that was last night, and now I know that was an act of mercy."

"What if it hadn't been?"

She sighed. "Then I don't know, Xavier. What I know is that I was permitted to live, and you have saved my life twice. You're not a monster for that. Even so, am I living, Xavier? I don't mean to seem ungrateful about you saving me that night, but what is the purpose of me being here? Really? How long do you think this will last? It feels like my death is being drawn out and that just makes me feel worse. Get it over with."

He didn't look away, but he didn't respond either. I hadn't meant to say so much, but once I started talking, I couldn't stop. Why should I stop anyway?

"And what you said that night in the kitchen was a real dick move. I'm going to punch you in the nuts for it one day."

His brow arched, and to my surprise, he began to smirk. It wasn't helping that he was freaking gorgeous right now, sitting there looking all cool and mysterious. Why was his smile growing?

He reclined, a full-blown smile on his face, but I made a face as that smile vanished as quickly as it had appeared.

"You're bipolar, aren't you?" I said. What had that smile meant?

"I'm sorry for what I said. I shouldn't have said that to you. No one, werewolf or human, deserves what almost happened to you. Get dressed."

I looked over at him as he got up and started walking towards the door. "What? Why?"

He opened the door before looking back at me and he sighed. "For once, Ruby, do as you're told and get dressed. Be ready in the next hour. I'm leaving, with or without you."

He slammed the door behind him as he left.

6

RUBY

*N*ow I understood how dogs felt when their owners decide to take them outside. I was out of the house! I was out of the house, and it wasn't for work. And while I didn't know where I was going, *I was excited*. I had gotten dressed as Xavier had demanded and had found him outside just as he was getting into his car.

The asshole really was going to leave without me.

I could feel eyes on me as I got into the car, but there was no one outside that I could see. For a moment my excitement faltered, my imagination painting a picture of wolves hidden in the trees watching me with vengeful eyes.

I sat back as Xavier pulled out, his matte black Audi speeding toward the large iron gates that led to my freedom. No matter how temporary it would be. I knew I would have to return to this place at the end of the day, but I sighed and pushed that thought away. I decided to just be in the moment.

During the long drive to the gate, I stared ahead at the towering trees that lined both sides of the driveway. I watched as the limbs swayed and a smile made its way onto my lips. I'd been trying to deny it, but being surrounded by nature is peaceful. I awaken every morning to a breathtaking view and the sound of birds. With the fast pace of the city left behind, I'm starting to appreciate nature's beauty a lot more.

"How many werewolves are in your pack? So far I've seen less than ten people."

"Fifty-two."

My eyes widened as I looked over at him. "Seriously? Wow. Where are they? Are there other houses here in the woods like yours?"

He held the steering wheel with one hand and my breath hitched as he reached over to me, his arm brushing against me. He grabbed my seatbelt and strapped me in without taking his eyes off the road.

I frowned, a churning in my gut. He smelled amazing.

"There are a few houses here in the woods, yes, but some wolves live in the city. Only a few though."

"Oh."

He pressed a button on his keychain and the gate swung open. We drove in silence for a couple of minutes before I was unable to hold it in any longer. "What's it like? Changing into a wolf?"

He didn't answer right away, and I held my breath waiting to see if he would. Mathieu had said I would learn from them, so I was going to ask every question that came to mind. I had originally planned to find Natalie, but for whatever reason, Xavier was being nice to me right now. I was going to take advantage of it.

"The first change is painful. It happens from a young age, between ten years old and thirteen. As we grow older, it becomes easier. You don't notice the pain anymore. Being a werewolf is like when you're sitting in an uncomfortable position and your leg falls asleep. You can feel your leg, but at the same time, you can't really feel it. I can feel that side of me there, under my skin."

I turned in my seat to face him, my interest piqued. "And when it comes out?"

"It feels like I'm truly myself. My leg isn't sleeping anymore, and I can feel it, truly feel it." His mouth twisted into a smile. "We already have heightened senses, but in wolf form, it becomes so much stronger. Everything becomes better."

"That sounds amazing."

His brow arched and he threw a look my way. "Does it?"

"Isn't it?" I countered. "To have such power and strength, it has to feel amazing."

He slowed the car for a stoplight and turned to look at me. "It's not always so. Some wolves hate being wolves because they have to keep so many secrets. We go to work and school and live alongside humans, but we have to hide so much, hide who we are. Living in a world like this with the abilities we have is hard. One slip-up and that's it, we go viral on YouTube." The light turned green and he drove off. "Yes, being a wolf is amazing, but it has its downsides."

He didn't say anything after that, and neither did I. I hadn't thought about the pressure wolves must feel trying to be normal, pretending to be something they're not just to remain safe. My mind took me back to last night, and I couldn't remove the image of the transformed wolves from my mind.

They were scary, but they were beautiful. But I knew not everyone would see that beauty.

He continued to drive quickly but confidently, and I sank into my seat, my mind taking me back to the story Natalie had told me. Yes, my heart would be shattered if I fell in love with a wolf, only to have him leave me for someone else. My heart would be shattered if a human left me for someone else, but I would never in a million years do what the princess in that story had done.

She could never have really loved that wolf if she played a part in killing him. Her love wasn't real. The man Xavier killed out of mercy had known love. I would probably never know what a mate bond felt like. What I know, however, is that for a bond like that to exist, even if it's meant to strengthen bloodlines, the unconditional love it creates between two wolves must be amazing.

Well, I'd think more about that later. For now, I still had more questions. "So, you guys don't need the full moon to transform, do you?"

Xavier shook his head as he turned into a parking lot. I hadn't even realized we were in the heart of the city. "No, we don't. We can change at will." He looked over at me and for a second his eyes were completely black, and my heart skipped a beat. "During a full moon, however, we can't transform."

"Wait, really? That's the complete opposite of what books and movies say."

He chuckled. "I know. My ancestors created that lie. During the full moon, we can't transform, and that's when our pregnant women give birth. A pup born outside of the three days surrounding a full moon can kill the mother. We're born in human form under the full moon, but outside of a full moon a pup is born as a real pup, a transformed wolf."

"Jesus," I said under my breath as I imagined a woman being ripped open by a baby wolf. "Have you ever seen that happen?"

He turned the car off. "No. I think that's more myth than fact. A child has never been born outside of a full moon, that I know of, anyway."

We got out of the car and made our way toward a restaurant I'd never seen before. It looked like a tavern you would find in the 1900s, and I was instantly intrigued. Its walls were made of wood with a large wooden sign hanging just above the door, "The Witches Brew" written on it in red paint.

"Wow." Since I hadn't even been in town a month yet, there were so many places in the city I had yet to see. Over a week ago, the thought of maybe never getting to see the city again would have made me angry, but I've fallen in love with the woods. Which I wasn't going to admit to anyone. However, I missed the sounds of the city, too. "I love this. Is this owned by a wolf?"

Xavier stepped ahead of me and pulled the door open. The way he looked down at me with a sly grin had my stomach doing backflips.

Damn, what is happening right now?

"I thought you might, and a witch actually; hence the name," he answered.

I paused, one foot inside the tavern. "Huh? A real witch?"

He nodded, and we stepped inside. As the door closed behind us, a bell rang above our heads. I felt like I'd been transported into the past. Just picture an old tavern from any movie you've watched, and you'd be spot on. The tables and chairs, the bar and shelves, were all solid handcrafted wood. The tavern was cloaked in semi-darkness, with only a single window above the door and a few dim lamps on each table. It was oddly cool inside as well.

There was a surprisingly large number of people inside. Xavier led me to the bar, and I hopped onto one of the wooden stools. I spotted a boy with a hoodie over his head in the corner of the room, his fingers dancing quickly over his laptop's keyboard. "Is there Wi-Fi in here?"

"Of course. We're not barbarians." My head whipped around to find a woman standing behind the counter with a towel thrown over her shoulder. "Well, not anymore."

She swiped at a strand of black hair that had come loose from her high bun. "The usual?" she asked Xavier, and he nodded. "And you, lass?"

I arched a brow. Who was she calling lass? Was she the witch who owned this tavern? She looked young, late 20s young, with sun-kissed skin and freckles over her nose.

"Whiskey."

She gave me a little smirk. "Whiskey at 11 a.m.–you're my kind of woman." She nodded and turned away.

I watched as she walked away, noticing that her left arm was completely covered in tattoos. They were all some form of writing in a language I did not recognize. "So, is she the witch?"

"Yeah, her name's Willow. She's been running this tavern since it opened in the 1600s."

Wow, I thought to myself. I wasn't too surprised, however. Since I now knew for sure that werewolves were real, I guess all other supernatural beings were probably real, too. I spun slowly around on my stool, my eyes darting over everyone sitting inside the tavern. I couldn't help wondering if they were humans or supernatural; maybe there was a blend of both.

The boy in the corner looked my way, and I stopped breathing. He had red pupils with vertical irises like a cat's.

"What is he?" I leaned in and whispered to Xavier. He merely glanced at the boy, and then looked away.

"He's a demon. I wouldn't keep staring if I were you. He's a dream demon. You don't want him latching onto you. They plague humans in their dreams, feeding off their fears."

I looked away instantly, but I could still feel those red eyes on me. "Everyone in here is supernatural?"

Xavier shook his head as Willow appeared with our drinks. "No lass," she said. There are humans here too, but they are none the wiser about the supernatural beings around them." She pointed at the boy with the red eyes. "He's a demon, a young one." She then pointed to the other end of the room where a girl with green hair was sipping on her drink and tapping at her phone. "That's a fae."

I arched a brow as the girl's eyes darted our way before she sniffed and looked back down at her phone.

"Hmm, rude," I said under my breath, and Willow chuckled.

"Yeah, fae aren't very friendly." She tilted her head to look at Xavier, and I saw a flash of violet in her brown eyes. "I'm curious to know why a wolf is hanging with a human, Xavier. Things have been boring around here lately. Why don't you give me the details so I can have a good gossip?"

I watched their interaction silently as Xavier took a sip of his drink before answering. "You'll find out one way or another. I'm not going to make things easy for your nosy ass."

She tossed her head back and laughed. "Fine." She looked my way, her eyes still violet, and I couldn't help leaning in closer, intrigued by the odd color. "You're a strange one, though." She looked me up and down. "A strange one."

What the hell did she mean by that? I mean, I've never been one to blend in with a crowd. I've always stood out because of my flaming red hair. But I could feel in my bones that she meant something other than my looks.

"What do you mean?"

She shrugged and turned away. "Holler when you're ready to pay the bill. I have an appointment in the back with a woman who says her dead husband is still trying to have sex with her."

Ruby

$\mathcal{X}$avier looked up and down the street before crossing, and I followed close by his side. After leaving The Witches Brew, we hadn't gotten back into his car. We left the parking lot, turned left, and had now been walking for ten minutes.

We hadn't really talked to each other during our walk, but it wasn't an uneasy silence. It felt comfortable. I felt protected. Was it because I knew about the power within him? I hadn't expected to be getting along with him so well.

Why did he offer to do this? Why be nice to me now? Was it all just because of his guilt over what he had said to me?

"So, supernatural creatures are all friendly with each other?"

"No, Ruby, they aren't all friendly with each other. Just like not all humans get along with each other." He tapped my shoulder for me to follow him and turned left. Ahead of us appeared a large fountain.

"Wow," I said under my breath. "I only just moved here for school. I didn't get the time to explore the city." When we finally stopped at the fountain, I dipped a finger and then my hand into the water. "Why did you do this? Why take me to that tavern and here? Why are you being kind to me now?"

I turned around to face him but was forced to take a step back. I hadn't realized he was so close to me. I frowned at the warmth that spread throughout my body. He took a step forward and I stepped back, but the back of my leg bumped the edge of the fountain.

I was trapped, but despite the intensity in his eyes, I didn't feel threatened. We were in public anyway, what did I think would happen? He'd wolf out right here in the open?

I crossed my arms over my chest, and he just smiled. "Do you mind?" I asked. "I can see your pores with how close you're standing."

"Do I make you nervous?"

I kept my face straight, but my nails were digging into my arms. "Do I look nervous to you? You're just invading my space, Blackwood."

He bent at the waist. "I can smell it," he whispered. He stood up straight as I started grinding my teeth, an impish smile on his face. "Don't worry, you smell good."

He was playing with me. That's what this had to be about. I watched him closely as he stepped around me to stand at the fountain's edge as well, the air alive with the splashing water.

"Despite what you might have thought, I don't hate you, Ruby." He dipped his hand into the water and scooped some of it up. "My life was calm until I met you." He slapped the water. "Now my life is like this, disrupted."

"If you were trying to say something nice, it's not going in that direction. I didn't mean to uproot your life, but my life has changed, too."

He turned to me and stepped closer, forcing me to look up into his eyes. "Is it so bad living at my house?"

Was he being serious?

"Um…" I exhaled and looked away at the clear glistening water, before looking up at a slowly drifting cloud. "No, it's not so bad. But it would be better if I wasn't living there and being kept on a short leash."

His hand brushed against mine, and a bolt of electricity shot up my arm, forcing me to step back. When I did, he grabbed my arm. I gasped and looked up at him, but the irritation on his face was only serving to confuse me. What was that feeling when he had touched me?

He reached out, and my body went stiff as he reached around me and grabbed my ponytail. I swallowed as he loosened my hair and pocketed my scrunchie. "I told you to let your hair down, didn't I? You're not on a short leash Ruby. You can come to the city. You can start going back to your classes. You can live a normal life."

"I can't take the constant stares…"

He frowned, and his hand fell away from my arm. The

spot he had been holding was no longer warm, and I wanted to tell him to hold me again.

Okay no, no. Slow down, Sonic the Hedgehog, you're moving way too fast right now.

I shook my head. "The few wolves I've seen look at me like they want to claw my eyes out. A girl flashed her fangs at me."

"What?" Xavier yelled, catching the eyes of two men walking by. He didn't spare them a glance, however; his anger was aimed at me, and I wasn't sure why he was so angry. After all, he was one of the people who were mean to me. "Who did that?"

"I don't know her name," I replied with irritation. "I do want to know more about you guys, and demons and witches and stuff. I want to know everything since I'm a part of this world now. However, it'll take some time to get used to living with people who hate me because I wasn't born special."

He inhaled deeply and rubbed a hand across his forehead. "Okay, look, when we get back, I'll give you a proper tour of the house and grounds and introduce you to a few people. Everyone just needs to get used to the idea of you being around and trust that you won't betray us."

"Do you trust that I won't betray you, Xavier?"

The world around us seemed to vanish as our eyes locked. Heaviness began to settle on my chest and my palms grew sweaty when he took a step closer to me. I felt faint suddenly, but I was unable to break eye contact. Since the moment we'd met, his eyes had been unreadable. Until now, and what I saw within them was frightening.

Raw, uncensored, desperate need.

He reached out and wrapped a strand of my hair around his finger. "I trust that you won't, Ruby."

I hadn't seen it coming, and I wasn't sure if he had seen it coming either, but when his lips pressed to mine I felt like a volcano erupted inside me. I leaned into his chest and the heat coming off him was staggering. Why was he so hot?

My fingers curled into his shirt as he pulled my bottom lip into his mouth and I caved into him, literally. He wrapped his arms around me and pulled me up and off the ground. Somewhere in my mind, a voice was yelling for me to push him away, but I couldn't. I felt drawn to him suddenly, more than I ever had. All thoughts of anything but here and now flew out of my head. Nothing was going to stop me from exploring this kiss. His lips tasted so good, his arms were so strong, and his body was so warm.

I pulled away first, the fog in my mind clearing, and he released me immediately. "I'm sorry," he said, his voice low, but he didn't sound apologetic.

"It's okay. Um, why did you do that?"

I wasn't complaining. *Oh no, most definitely not!* I'd never been kissed like that in my entire life. But why had it happened, why had it felt so good? Like an acid flashback, I remembered Natalie's story about the tragic end of a were-wolf and human relationship and I took a step away from him.

Oh no.

"Um, actually, that just now, it never happened. Okay?" I turned and walked away, my legs like jelly. "We should head back to the house. I want that tour."

What the fuck did I just let happen?

Ruby

The drive back to the house was a quiet one, and this time the radio blasted to cover the awkward silence. Xavier had kissed me, and I had let him. I wasn't sure how I'd face him after this. I couldn't even handle turning my head to look in his direction. Why had he done that?

I thought he'd never dated a human, from what Natalie had said that day in the library. I had been convinced he wasn't even attracted to *my kind.* So why, out of all the women throwing themselves at him, did he decide to stick his tongue down my throat?

My day had been going so well. He had been on the brink of making me think this could all work out, and then he had to ruin it. My life before this hadn't been perfect. My life has never even been close to perfect. My financial worries had disappeared since being forced to live here. Despite how nerve-wracking this had all been, I was slowly falling in love with the woods, but now I'd give it up in a heartbeat with no second thought. *Xavier had kissed me. This could end badly!*

I'm no longer the human girl being allowed to live, but the human girl Xavier kissed. If that's not a can of worms, I don't know what is.

I bit down on my lip as the gates leading to the house opened. No, I was lying to myself. Sure, werewolves exist, and so do demons; but I was one of the few, perhaps the only, human in a position to know about this hidden world. Sure, it would take some time to get settled, but I was going to make the best of this. A kiss wouldn't ruin that.

I groaned inwardly.

An already awkward situation was just made ten times worse.

We pulled up to the entrance of the house and Xavier got out before I did. As I opened my door a loud crash could be heard inside the house. I glanced over at Xavier. With his heightened senses, it seemed he could hear what was going on, and his face was turning red with rage.

What's going on?

The front door flew open and a man's booming angry voice met my ears. My body tensed when I could finally make out the words he yelled.

"Where the FUCK is she?!"

Faster than my eyes could track, something bolted out of the front door and slammed into Xavier. Within the next second, Natalie appeared by my side, but my eyes were glued to Xavier and the man who attacked him.

The men pulled apart, both rolling in opposite directions before getting to their feet. Xavier's claws were elongated, his eyes black pits of rage, but when I looked at his attacker my face twisted as a wave of nausea slammed into me. Hazel eyes were piercing into my green ones, and my body started to feel hot.

Natalie grabbed my arm as I staggered backward, my hand slowly rising to clutch at my chest. I felt like the world was caving in on me. I groaned and doubled over as the hazel-eyed man growled and his eyes turned black.

He attacked Xavier, the sound of them fighting only making me feel worse. Why was I getting sick right now?

"Stop them!" I yelled as Mathieu appeared on my other side. "What's going on?" The man swiped at Xavier and his claws dug into Xavier's side. "Stop!"

No one was listening to me. No one was even trying to stop the fight as Xavier grabbed the man by the throat and threw him down. More people were appearing around us, no doubt hearing the fight, but no one was doing anything.

The man got to his feet, and my skin started to burn as he looked my way. A surge of pain racked my body, and Natalie's hold on my arm grew tighter. I looked down at my open palms as they began to shake violently before looking at the newcomer again, Xavier's blood dripping from his claws.

My body suddenly felt numb, my legs growing weak.

"You have no right to keep her! Release her to me!" The man yelled as he looked Xavier's way, his body shaking with rage as he spoke.

Who was he talking about? Was he talking about *me*? I don't even know this man. Was he a part of the Council? Had they found out Mathieu was keeping a human pet? What the fuck is going on?

"I have every right to keep Ruby, and she's on my land." Xavier growled back, "You have no claim to her!"

Xavier seemed to have said the wrong words because the man fell to the ground and I watched as the back of his shirt began to rip. He was changing, right before my eyes. His skin was tearing and opening, blood pouring from his body as his nails dug into the ground. I've never seen a wolf transform and seeing it now was making my stomach turn. Why had no one told me it's as if the wolf is literally bursting from their body?

Vomit was rising to my throat quickly, my chest feeling

heavy with it, but it stopped, along with the rest of the world, when the stranger spoke once more, his voice deep and contorted.

"I have all rights because she's my mate! Release her!"

A chorus of gasps could be heard around us and Mathieu stepped forward, finally showing some concern. At first, he hadn't seemed concerned that his son was battling, possibly to the death, with this clearly deranged man. But what the fuck had he just said?

I'm his mate?

No, no, this has to be a joke. He's a werewolf, I'm a human. Who is this man?

Mathieu stepped before me, his large body blocking me, and to my surprise, they both growled at him.

"Ruby can't be released to you. She's not just your mate, she's Xavier's as well."

Oh no, the fuck I'm not!

Pain blossomed within my gut, and I hugged myself as I leaned forward. "You're all crazy," I said. But before I could properly finish the sentence I vomited, my body shaking violently as I fell to the ground.

The world around me blurred as the two men rushed my way, but I was consumed by darkness before they could get to me.

7

RUBY

I could hear muffled voices through the darkness around me, but I was comfortable. I didn't want to give in and wake up. I wanted to remain asleep, swaddled in the warmth around me.

I wanted to tell the voices to be quiet, but my eyes cracked open regardless. The talking around me stopped. I groaned as I swallowed. My tongue felt like sandpaper against the roof of my mouth, and I sat up, rubbing at my temples.

"You're awake."

No shit, can I go back to sleep?

That's what I wanted to say to Xavier, but I remained quiet. The moment I had opened my eyes, I remembered some of what had happened. I just wasn't sure if everything I remembered was from reality or a dream. I inhaled deeply and swung my legs off the sofa to curl my toes on the cool marble floor, my eyes wandering from Xavier to Mathieu. Xavier was standing beside the chair Mathieu was sitting in.

Mathieu crossed his legs, his steady eyes watching my every move.

I preferred sleeping forever over facing what I'm about to.

"What did your father mean when he said I'm your mate, Xavier?"

My eyes flicked to him, and he shifted uncomfortably "I told you about mates. That is what we are. What you are to me. That's why you weren't killed."

I started laughing. I wasn't sure why, but the laughter bubbled to the surface, and I could not hold it in. He was joking. There was no way I was his mate. But they didn't look amused.

I sobered up, and a feeling of foreboding settled on my shoulders.

"You're serious? You can't be serious!"

"A mate can't be harmed," Mathieu said calmly. I sat back, sinking into the sofa's cushions. "Under any circumstances. There has just never been a human mate before. We needed to handle this delicately."

"Delicately? Delicately as in keeping me here by telling me some crap about learning from each other. I knew that didn't make any sense. Why did no one tell me about this?" I looked at Xavier, my rage growing greater by the minute. "How long did the two of you plan on keeping this a secret? This affects my life too." I leaned forward and covered my face with my hands. "This can't be real."

"That's enough, Ruby. It's real, and you need to accept it."

I looked up slowly. I didn't care if Mathieu could kill me with little effort, he was pissing me off. "With all due respect,

Mr. Blackwood, don't tell me I need to accept this. I'm not from this world. I just fell into this world! Now I'm his mate? Can you give me a minute to catch up?" I pointed at Xavier and shook my head as I stood up. "You're both lying." My hand fell to my side limply. "You're lying," I said more softly. Xavier took a step toward me but stopped himself from taking another.

He crossed his arms over his chest. Despite the sternness on his face, I could see regret within his eyes. "It's why you got sick the first time we were close to each other. You felt our bond."

His jaw clenched, and my shoulders slumped as I lost what little strength I had to argue with him. Of course, he must be affected by this as well, but why keep a secret like this from me? Sooner or later it would be revealed. So why wait? This was all becoming too much for me.

My face smoothed out, the crease between my brows vanishing. That's why he had kissed me. That's why he had lost his cool that night and saved me. It all made sense now.

He inhaled, and the sudden irritation on his face caused my fading anger to return. If anyone had the right to be irritated right now, it was me. "So you've been planning this since then? That's what you're saying?"

"No. What happened that night wasn't supposed to happen, Ruby. Things were set into motion too quickly. We knew this would be too much for you to handle right now, with you just getting settled here. I figured, maybe if you learned to be comfortable here, telling you that you and I were mates wouldn't be such a devastating blow.

"I couldn't have you leaving the pack. If this were to get to the Council's ears before we had more information, you'd be unprotected out there. None of this was planned.

The day you met Natalie in the library, I picked up your scent on her. That's how I found you. But I didn't say anything to her until I visited the diner with her. Your scent seemed off when I had smelled it on her, but I hadn't given it much thought until I saw you and you turned out to be human. That's why you got sick when I saw you. A mate bond being discovered is different for wolves, though. They feel it more. They feel a deep connection or pull between them and their partner, but it doesn't make them sick."

He exhaled as if he had been holding his breath, and my headache grew worse. No wonder he had looked so pissed that day.

Natalie has known all this time as well, and she said nothing!

"This has to be a trick. This has to be a witch's doing."

I spun around to find the stranger who had attacked Xavier leaning on the wall by the door. My sanity was hanging on by a thread here. He was real, the fight was real. So does that mean… No, I can't be his mate, too!

I looked around at Xavier, at the way he was staring daggers at the man, and I finally noticed his ripped shirt and the dried blood on it. I clenched my fists as I looked at the stranger once more.

He was wearing a black leather jacket with his arms crossed over his chest like Xavier. He was taller, however, and more muscular, with a brown complexion and long curly hair tied back in a low ponytail. Where Xavier was refined and polished, he was rougher and more roguish, and he had a leaf earring dangling from his ear.

With everything now calm, I could really stare at him. The dislike that I had for Xavier in the beginning was nothing compared to the disgust in this guy's eyes as he looked at me.

He looked older, mid-twenties maybe. But was that right? Mathieu looked to be in his mid-thirties and I was sure he was older. Was Xavier even twenty-two years old?

"This girl can't be real." He looked me up and down, and I made a face. "A wolf can't have a human mate, let alone the same mate as another wolf. Not even wolves can have two mates. She's a witch." His hazel eyes narrowed at me, and I looked back at him with same intensity.

"I'm standing right in front of you, so I'm as real as your attitude, and I'm not a witch. Don't worry, I share your disgust, but don't speak as if I'm not standing right here."

He growled at me. In response, I raised a brow and placed my hands on my hips. This guy didn't scare me. Okay, who was I kidding? I was terrified. But he didn't need to know that. He pushed himself off the wall, not satisfied that I hadn't cowered in fear at his little growl. I held my ground as he came closer.

Behind me, Xavier growled, and the stranger stopped in his tracks. "Axel, that's close enough."

Axel.

I narrowed my eyes at him and held my head up. He sneered and unfolded his arms. "I don't have time for this. The mouthy little secret is out now..." I frowned. Who was he calling mouthy? "And the Council is going to hear about it."

Did this fucker just call me "it"?!

He looked Mathieu's way, and his spine straightened as he did so. I was only human, but even I could feel the waves of dominance that radiated off him. Like Mathieu. Was this man an alpha?

"You're fools to think they don't have people placed in your pack solely to watch and report. I don't want any part of this." He looked me up and down again. This time he smiled, but it looked more like an evil sneer to me. "But I think this problem will solve itself. If she isn't claimed by time the Council finds out, we'll both be forced to reject her, and then she'll die anyway."

Natalie

I closed my eyes as I listened to Ruby's soft sobs. I could tell she was trying to be quiet since she knew she could easily be heard. If I hadn't come to her door, I wouldn't have heard her crying. Instead of knocking, I pulled the door open slowly and entered the room.

With the evening sun lighting the room I easily found her. She was face down on her bed with her face pressed into one pillow and another pillow over her head. I sighed as I approached her bed and sat down. Despite her heart skipping a beat from her fright, she didn't physically jump. She fell silent, and I waited for her to sit up. When she didn't, I tapped her leg.

"Ruby, it's only me." She sat up then, the pillow on her head falling to the floor, and I could see her swollen and bloodshot eyes. "I'm so sorry."

"You could have told me," she said weakly, and I shook my head.

"I couldn't, babe. Alpha's orders. But I wish I could have." I reached out to smooth down her hair, but she suddenly swatted at my hand. I quickly pulled it away.

"You've known all this time, Natalie. You've known I'm Xavier's mate all this time. You all made me think one day I might die, instead of simply telling me I'm Xavier's mate and can't be touched." She chuckled and hung her head. "But even that won't save me. Axel said I'll die when they both reject me. Is Axel really my mate as well?"

I nodded. It had been a shock to everyone when he had arrived for a meeting with Mathieu only to go ballistic after smelling Ruby. Mathieu had tried to calm him, but it had been no use because Xavier returned with her at that very moment.

"He is,"

She slid down to the edge of the bed and sat beside me. When we had first met, there had been this spunk to her, a refreshing attitude. Now it was gone. "Every time my life seems to be making a change for the better, something goes wrong. Maybe both men should reject me, let me die because at this point I don't want to know what's going to happen next."

I picked her hand up and squeezed it gently. "Over my dead body. He only said that because rejection is pretty harmful to a wolf, and if you get sick from just the mate bond being discovered," I made a face, "we think you might die from rejection. Everyone is as confused as you are, honestly; there has never been a human mate. Imagine a piece of string getting knotted. You try to unknot it, but you can't, so the string snaps. That's what rejection is like for a wolf, a bond gets ripped apart. That won't just be hurtful to you, but to the guys, too. The rejected feels it more than the rejecter."

Her voice was low and shaking as she said, "That does sound horrible. I saw Xavier kill that man who had lost his mate. It seems to me with wolves there is just too much that can hurt them." A sad smile appeared on her lips as she moved her hair to one shoulder. "I must be crazy for feeling sorry for Xavier and Axel if either one of them has to go through that. Well, Xavier more than Axel. I don't even know the guy, or like him."

"You just met him, and you didn't like Xavier at first either."

She arched a brow and turned to face me. "Why do you sound like you're on Axel's side, or sympathizing with him or something?"

"Trust me, I'm not. But at the end of the day, he *is* your mate, Ruby. If you don't feel anything for him now, you will. And no matter how much of a dick he might be, he doesn't hate you."

I think.

I have yet to find my mate, and honestly, it's not something I'm excited about. I've never been good with romantic relationships.

She just grunted and fell backward. "Yeah, you didn't see the way he looked at me." Her head lolled to the side, and I leaned down and propped my head on my hand. "Tell me about him, who is he?" she asked.

"He's Axel Grimmwolf. Like Xavier, he's next in line to be alpha. His pack and ours have been rivals for a while. His pack split from ours decades ago. I don't know why, but there has been bad blood for years." I took a deep breath and lay down beside her. No one was going to walk away from this unscathed. I could feel in my bones that a storm was coming. "He was here for a meeting with Mathieu. But while things have been peaceful enough, I think this may have just changed everything. Axel and his pack aren't like ours. They despise humans and are ruthless. To be honest, I can't be sure he won't try to hurt you."

"Now more than ever I won't be able to leave the house, huh?"

I nodded. "Xavier won't want you out of his sight. He might become overbearing, but try to understand why he's protective of you. You're not feeling the pull from the bond like he is. Axel said there might be a spy in our pack for the Council, but that spy was found a long time ago. The Council won't hear about you from us, but now we have Axel to worry about. It's more likely that Axel will reject you than Xavier will, and we don't know what that'll do to you yet. So for now," I gave her the sternest expression I could, "don't leave the grounds unaccompanied."

She rolled onto her stomach, and I did the same, watching her as she pressed her face into the pillow. We stayed like that in silence for a moment and I heard a wolf howling in the distance. It was too far for Ruby to hear it, but I knew it was Xavier.

I couldn't imagine the stress and worry he was now walking around with. He's the son of an alpha, and he'll soon be the alpha, which would make Ruby the pack's luna. No doubt he was worried about the impact that would have; a human as a luna is ludicrous.

"I should have seen something like this coming." Ruby's words were muffled before she turned her head to lie on her cheek. I could see the fresh tears she was desperately trying to hold back. "Things are only going to get worse from here on in. I just know it."

8

RUBY

*C*olorful leaves floated down around me as I walked through the woods. I figured with the pack now knowing that I'm Xavier's mate, I could walk around more freely without thinking someone might kill me.

I was sure the moment I ran into any wolves I'd still get cold stares, but honestly, I wasn't so bothered anymore. I had more important things to think about, like Axel jumping out from behind a tree to reject me.

I needed fresh air. I couldn't handle being trapped in the house another second with my chaotic thoughts, not after what had happened yesterday.

So here I was, out of the house, following a path I had noticed a few days ago. The woods around me were filled with the melodic calls of birds and the wind whistling in the trees above me. I needed this. I needed a moment alone to collect my thoughts and try to piece everything together.

I'm Xavier's mate.

I smiled as I bent down to pick a flower and secure it behind my ear. I then ran a finger over my lips as I remembered the way his lips had felt against mine, the way I had fit so perfectly in his arms. I now understood why I had given in to that kiss so easily, why my body had seemed to crave more and more of his touch the longer we had been pressed together.

Ever since Natalie and I talked yesterday I haven't been able to stop wondering what it's like for him to have found me. For me, all I had felt was nausea. But what had gone through his mind the moment he had smelled me on Natalie and had known that, whoever this person was, she was his soulmate?

Natalie had said wolves are territorial, so no wonder he had lost his mind and killed those men who attacked me in the alleyway. He had only just found his mate and had to deal with seeing her in danger of being raped.

Voices on the wind made me stop in my tracks, but there was no one in sight. I looked behind me. I couldn't see Xavier's house anymore.

Shit.

I took a deep breath and strained my ears, wishing I had a werewolf's super-hearing to tell me if I should be running for my life. Instead, I heard laughter and decided to leave the path to see what was happening. It didn't take five minutes before an opening appeared ahead of me.

There was a two-story house and in front of it were seven men and three women, all training. Some were lifting weights, others were stretching. My heart skipped a beat as I saw the rest of the group circling Xavier as he sparred with another man.

He was shirtless, his body glistening in the sun with the sweat covering his body. His hair was damp and sticking to his neck and forehead. I drew closer and took a seat as he and the other man charged at each other and began fighting.

He caught the man in a headlock and then released him. I watched as he explained the move to the onlookers, all of them nodding with understanding, their eyes glued to Xavier.

"So, you're the redhead I've been hearing about."

I looked over my shoulder to find a man with similar red hair to mine grinning down at me. His hair was curly and covered his ears and forehead. He wasn't as bulky as the other men I'd seen around. However, he was smiling at me, and that was a pleasant surprise.

"That's me," I replied, and he walked closer to sit next to me on the log I had claimed for my seat.

He stuck his hand out to me. "The name's Randoll. I'm the beta for this pack." I shook his hand while looking at him skeptically and he chuckled. "Don't worry, I don't bite. It's nice you're getting out of the house."

"Is it?" I asked as I turned my attention back to Xavier, who was now fighting with someone else, a girl with a blonde bob.

"It is," Randoll replied. "Wouldn't you prefer to show who you really are yourself, or would you prefer to have them make up their own stories about you instead? So far, you're just the human at the alpha's house. Well, now we know you're not just a human." He made a sound and I glanced over at him to see his freckle-covered nose scrunched up. "Then again, that has only caused more whispers about you."

This guy was a talker, but that was good. He looked like he'd be happy to tell me anything.

"Is that so? Like what?"

He shrugged. "That you're a witch. That you were created by a witch. Just a lot of witch rumors, honestly."

"I met a witch, Willow. She seemed nice, but I'm starting to get the idea that werewolves and witches aren't friends."

He drummed his hands against his thighs and nodded. "Have you heard about the Salem witch trials? Werewolves helped humans with that massacre. Of course, that was years ago. But hatred and grudges like that are passed down through generations, you know."

"I see." I watched Xavier step away from the group to check on the other wolves who were exercising, and I smiled as he showed one guy the right way to do push-ups. Everyone's eyes were glued to him, and I could understand why. He was obviously skilled, and his movements were fluid.

"So, is it true you're mated to Axel as well? I wasn't there yesterday to see the fight, but news travels fast around here. These morons don't know what it means to capture something as epic as that on video."

I looked over at him and found him already staring at me intently. "Yes," I said as I narrowed my eyes, and to my surprise, he started grinning. "Why are you laughing?"

"That's insane. That's never happened before! Not even to a wolf, and now two wolves have a human mate. The same mate! So, tell me, what was your reaction when you found out about us, that werewolves are real?"

"I was freaked out, yes, but I was also curious to know more, you know? There is a world around humans that we can't see, even though it's right before our eyes."

"So, you didn't get the urge to hunt us with silver knives or anything like that?"

I couldn't help smiling at his face-splitting grin. What was with this guy?

"No, of course not. Why would I do that? You're not monsters to be hunted." His grin flattened for a moment, and I looked down at my hands. "You're people, just like me. You all belong on this earth, just like me. Why discriminate against you all just because you're stronger and faster. That's just jealousy."

"Something humans have in abundance."

I laughed. I liked this guy. He was like the male version of Natalie, although he seemed a little more animated. "Yeah, I know."

I looked up and found a few wolves looking our way, but Xavier's back was turned as he spoke to another wolf. I had forgotten that they could all hear me clearly, and surely now they could hear by my heartbeat that I was panicking because of their sudden attention.

Randoll placed his hand over mine, and my head whipped his way. "You're not what I expected, Ruby." I smiled at him gratefully.

In the distance, a loud growl could be heard. Randoll rolled his eyes and didn't even look. I started looking around frantically only to find Xavier staring daggers at Randoll. His shoulders were moving up and down with his heavy breathing, and a few wolves stepped away from him.

What's his problem?

"So," I drawled as I tore my eyes away from Xavier. "This Council I keep hearing about, what's up with that?"

"Hmm. Humans have a government and wolves have a Council. There are three Council members, so the world is split into three. One governs all of Asia and so on. You get the gist."

I removed the flower that was behind my ear and let it fall to the ground. "Yeah, so fat old men who think they're the shit."

Randoll almost rolled off the log as he busted out laughing. The collar of his shirt shifted to the side, and I squinted my eyes at a faint scar there. Were those teeth marks?

"I really like you, Ruby."

We both looked toward the wolves who were training as a loud crash echoed through the forest. Thick silence followed Xavier dropping two dumbbells, and my eyes widened at seeing they were broken. The wolves around him all looked between him, Randoll, and me.

Seriously, what's his deal?

"That's my cue," Randoll mumbled beside me, and he got up the moment Xavier started heading our way.

"Wait, where are you going?" I yelled to him, but he only waved goodbye over his shoulder.

"I like my life, ma'am. I'll see you around, he's all yours."

When I looked around Xavier was already standing in front of me, his eyes narrowed and his bare chest rising and falling rapidly. He was upset, I could tell, but I wasn't sure why. Was he mad that I was talking to Randoll? I scoffed inwardly. He couldn't be.

Sure, he's my mate, but we aren't together. My eyes slid to the side with that thought, and it suddenly hit me that actually we were. We might not have verbally committed to each other, but if I'm his mate, we're in a relationship, right?

What about Axel?

He threw his shirt over his shoulder, but before he could

sit beside me I reached up and grabbed his wrist. He looked at my hand around his wrist as if it was burning his flesh, his eyes growing dark, and I quickly released him.

"Um, can we talk?" I peeped behind him at the wolves who had all gone back to training, "In private?"

He held his hand out to me, and without hesitation, I slid my hand into his. "Come."

He pulled me up, and I regretfully let go of him. He looked down at me for a moment, his breathing much slower, but I couldn't meet his eyes. I couldn't handle his naked chest, slicked with sweat, being in my face. The corner of his mouth twitched as if he knew what I was thinking, and then he turned away.

Weirdo.

We walked into the trees, but I kept silent by his side until we came upon a rocky cliff. I stopped walking when we got close to the edge, but he walked a few more steps before realizing I had stopped.

"What's wrong?"

"I'd rather not get too close to the edge."

He returned to my side. "I thought you feared nothing," he said as he laid his shirt on the ground and pointed at it. "Sit."

I sat down and crossed my legs lotus style. He sat down beside me, long legs stretched out as he leaned back on his hands.

"What made you think that?

He dropped his head back and closed his eyes. "You slapped a werewolf. I'd think only a person without fear would do that."

I jabbed a finger into his side, and he yelped and covered

the spot with a hand. "Be quiet." He smiled and his eyes cracked open. "So, are you okay?" I asked.

He closed his eyes once more. "I am."

"Yeah, I don't think the dumbbells you just killed would agree." He didn't say anything or even move, and I turned my body to face him. "Come on Xavier, you're my mate." His eyes cracked open. "You can't be okay with knowing that I also apparently belong to someone else."

He sat up then, and I was struck once more by his beauty. He reached out and tugged on the bun in my hair and watched as my hair tumbled down and over my shoulders. My body grew tense, my heartbeat hammering in my ears, as he inhaled deeply. I knew he was inhaling my scent.

"You're mine, Ruby, no one else's. Remember that."

Now if any other guy had said that to me, I would have punched him in the face. That sounded too much like I was an object to be owned. And while I felt the urge to tell Xavier he was dead wrong about that, I also liked the sound of it.

"I don't care that you're human. The goddess made you my mate, and she doesn't make mistakes. I trust my goddess, but I do have to wonder what the hell she's thinking making you Axel's mate as well." He finger-combed his damp hair backward.

"So, there is someone I can blame for this mess then? What goddess are you talking about?"

He smiled as he looked up at the sky, his eyes following the darkening clouds. "You'll learn about her soon enough. I used to come here every day at sunset and stay until the moon came up. The moon from this spot always looks like it's in reach." He grew serious and his jaw clenched tightly. "I won't let anything happen to you, Ruby. I hope you know that. That's why I've been thinking about taking you to an old Enchanted. She's like Natalie, although way more powerful."

I liked the sound of that. "When can we go?"

"Soon, and hopefully she'll be able to tell us how a human is mated to two wolves. I'll need to let her know we're coming because if the Council finds out about you they'll try to kill you. I have a bad feeling, Ruby, especially about Axel, and my feelings are never wrong."

"Natalie told me his pack hates humans."

He said nothing, but he didn't have to. I could see it on his face. I pulled my knees up to my chest and watched as the grass and flowers around us swayed in the light wind. "Yeah. I'm sorry about all of this," I said.

He cupped my cheek and turned my head toward him. I stopped breathing as his thumb began to move over my cheek. A feeling of belonging blossomed inside me and my eyes fluttered closed as I relaxed into his touch. His thumb glided over my lips and my eyes opened to see him leaning forward, his voice so husky the hairs on my arms stood on end. "Don't be sorry. You have nothing to be sorry about."

He kissed me gently, his lips barely touching mine, but the electricity that surged through my body could power a small city. He had kissed me chastely, but I could feel his emotions in that simple touch.

"I want to see you in your wolf form," I whispered against his lips, and he pulled away but kept his hand on my cheek. "I want to see the real you."

He leaned forward and pressed his lips to my forehead as thunder rumbled in the distance. "You will, but not today. It's going to start raining soon." He stood up and held his hand out to me. "We need to head back."

"So, are you going to carry me on your back or what?"

Ruby

*M*y fingers glided along the railing of the staircase as I made my way downstairs. Amid the chaos that is my life, I've found a reason to smile.

I wasn't entirely sure what was between Xavier and me, but after the day I had with him, I was eager to find out. I was petrified of Axel and the Council and the future in general, but in the here and now I had a reason to be happy.

For the first time in a long time, I wasn't being swept away by sadness or thoughts of dying, but from the memory of Xavier's lips on mine. Where my appetite had been off for a while, it had decided to return at 1 a.m. this morning.

I finished my sandwich, did the dishes, and was having a glass of water when a girl walked into the kitchen and took a seat at the island. I recognized her as the girl who had accompanied Xavier the day at the diner.

Why is she wearing a full face of makeup at 1 a.m.?

"You're not his mate."

I inhaled and placed my glass into the sink. I knew sooner or later someone would no longer hide behind their stares and whispers and speak up. "Oh really?"

"Yes, really. You're a weak human, that's all you are. You're not special, and you're not Xavier's mate. You will never be luna."

I smiled and I rested my elbows on the island. "What's your name again? Anna, right? Tell me something, Anna. What did you think was going to happen? You do realize if I'm not Xavier's mate, it still won't be you? Right?"

I walked away and she hopped off the stool to block my way out of the kitchen. Her eyes changed to black as she took a step closer to me, mere inches between us.

"I don't trust you, bitch." She growled. "I'll be right here when Xavier rejects you."

Who did this bitch think she was talking to? I might be human, but I wasn't going to give her the satisfaction of scaring me. She might be a werewolf, but I've met her kind before.

"It's funny how you're not getting it through your thick skull that no matter what happens, you will *never* be luna. I'm not going to fight you for something that I don't even want. Unlike you, I hold no delusions. If I don't become luna, it's not the end of my world. But whether I do or not, it'll be the end of yours. I might not know what being a luna really means, but I can tell right away you're not it. You're being a bitch about a title and a man who will never be yours, honey. Have some self-respect." I flipped my hair over my shoulder and stepped to the side so we were shoulder to shoulder. "Put your fangs away before you hurt yourself."

I walked away and didn't spare a glance backward as I made my way to my room, my bare feet absorbing the cold from the tile. Girls like her exist in all species, I was certain of it. I refrained from stomping my way up the stairs, pissed that she had ruined my good vibes. When I got to the landing of the second floor and glanced out the window, I spotted a man outside.

I looked more carefully, and my eyes widened as he removed his shirt and I realized it was Xavier. I arched a brow as he bent his head from side to side and then rolled his shoulders.

"What the hell are you doing?"

I looked down at my bare feet and then back through the window as he vanished into the dark forest.

"Damn it."

I ran back downstairs and headed outside, the cold air instantly nipping at my exposed legs. I didn't have the time to run to the third floor to get shoes or I'd lose sight of him completely.

The damp cold grass felt nasty between my toes, but I kept walking slowly through the trees, my eyes squinting, nothing but the moon's light keeping me from tripping and falling onto my face.

This was a bad idea. Xavier can navigate the darkness and he's more likely to be the predator out here than the prey. I was the prey.

What sounded like a large branch breaking startled me and a twig grabbed at my arm as I spun around. I hissed and held my hand up to see a small scratch when I heard another branch break.

Xavier is out here, so if anything jumps out of the bushes at me, I'll scream and he'll save me.

I sank my teeth into my lip as I went in the direction of the snapping branches and soon I could hear groaning. My heartbeat sped up, wondering if it was Xavier and if he could be hurt or wounded. I started walking faster, swatting at the bushes and branches that seemed to be reaching out to me, when suddenly something stumbled into my path.

I jumped back, a scream on my lips, but I swallowed it as I realized it was Xavier. Or at least I thought it was. The werewolf before me was bigger than the ones I had seen, eight feet tall maybe. I stepped back and the creature's head tilted to the side.

I froze, my chest rising and falling rapidly. Seeing those werewolves through a window at a distance was nothing compared to what I was seeing now. The creature tilted its head to the other side and my breath hitched.

"Xavier?" He made a sound like a snort and my need to piss myself vanished. "Gods, you scared me!"

He took a step closer and this time I didn't step back. He made another sound and raised his head to sniff the air before looking down at me once more.

"I saw you from inside the house. I just wanted to see what you were up to."

He suddenly fell onto all fours, and I jumped, a small yelp leaving my lips. He walked forward until I could feel his hot breath on me. Even on all fours, he still towered over me. I took my time admiring him. His fur was light brown with white running from under his chin to his chest.

His tail began to swish behind him, and I moved to the side, my eyes darting from his obsidian ones to his tail. I circled him until I reached his other side, and I held my breath as I reached a hand out.

His tail smacked my thigh, and he snorted through his nose as he quickly moved away.

Is he playing with me right now?

"Be nice or you won't get to kiss me ever again," I said. He growled and I pointed a finger at him. "Don't growl at me."

He shook his head and began sniffing as he came closer

once more. I lifted my hand, and he pressed his forehead to it. I closed my eyes as he pushed forward, like a dog begging to be petted, and I shoved my hand into his fur. It was soft and smooth. My body stiffened as he pressed his snout to my chest and inhaled.

"Hey!" I said as sternly as I could muster, but I didn't mind. If anything, I liked it.

I was standing under the half-moon with a werewolf, with my mate, and any onlooker would yell at me to run for my life. But I've never felt safer, barefoot in the woods and all.

He circled me and laid on the ground, his eyes on me almost expectantly. I barely hesitated before sitting beside him and nestling myself into his side. His body was radiating so much heat I soon began to feel drowsy. I must have fallen asleep for a minute because I was jolted awake to find Xavier shifting back into human form.

First, his shoulder snapped, and then his neck. I blinked rapidly, my eyes wide until he was fully human again. He smiled and combed my hair back from my face. I was trying hard not to look at his naked torso.

I started to blush, and his smile widened into a devilish one.

"Stay here with me for a while. I'll be right back. My clothes are in those bushes." He leaned forward and rubbed his nose against my shoulder, and I swear my body started to melt. "I'll keep you warm."

9

RUBY

*T*he more the night had progressed the darker it had gotten, but I knew that wasn't a problem for Xavier. He could see and hear things I couldn't, and he had made a show of having me stand directly in front of him as his eyes transformed to his wolf's eyes, black like the darkness around us. Since I had run out of the house barefoot, I finally got that piggyback ride from him as we made our way back to the house.

I pressed my cold cheek to his warm shoulder as my body swayed with each step he took.

With my eyes closed, I could see him within my mind, the real him. I smiled as I remembered the feeling of his fur between my fingers and his warm body at my back when I had lain beside him. The sudden onslaught of feelings confused me. Were they ours, or was my bond to him creating them? If there was no bond between us, would I still find him attractive? Because if the answer to that is no, my feelings couldn't be real.

Who was I kidding? I had found him attractive from the

moment I had laid eyes on him in that library. Sure, at the time I only thought he was hot, just not my type, as I had judged his personality without even knowing him.

I wrapped my hands a little tighter around his neck. "What was it like? When you smelled me on Natalie. What happened to you?"

He stepped over a broken branch. "Usually in human form, you can't feel your wolf," he began. "You know it's there, just under your skin, but you can't feel it the way you do when you call it forward to transform. When I smelled you, my wolf awakened on its own. The hairs on my body stood on end, and I felt as though if I didn't find you I'd rip the world apart."

"In the diner, when you got angry, it's because you saw that I was human. I'm human, and no matter the bond we have, I can never be luna. That puts you in a complicated position." I swallowed. "You'll have to reject me."

"A luna is the woman who stands by her alpha's side and offers him strength. A luna has always been a wolf, but there is nothing in our laws that says a luna can't be from another species."

I scoffed at that. "I think that's because it's a given that it can only be a wolf."

"Ruby, I won't reject you and I won't step away from one day being the alpha of this pack. You don't have to take on the duties of being the luna. My dad has been running the pack on his own for years. My mom's passing took a toll on him, but being the alpha, he *had* to pull through."

I frowned. "He didn't end up like the man you killed?"

I could hear the pain in his voice as he replied. "Almost. Something like that takes a toll on a wolf, but some more than others." He cleared his throat and I made a mental note to ask him about his mother another time. I had noticed Mathieu's wedding ring but the lack of a mate. "The point is, a luna is important, but not mandatory for a pack's survival."

"So, it's like cereal tasting better with milk, but you can still eat it without."

He chuckled and nodded his head. "Yes, exactly, but you don't have to worry about any of that right now. One step at a time. That means contacting the Enchanted as soon as possible."

I knew the thought of losing me was painful to Xavier; I could hear it in his voice whenever the topic of losing a mate arose. I was just as scared of dying as I had been when I first came here, but now I simply couldn't stand the thought of what might happen to him if I… No, no, I won't think like that.

No one knows the future, but I had to believe I wouldn't die this young. However, I hadn't been able to get what Axel had said out of my mind. What if I really was created by a witch? But to do what, exactly? In a world of the impossible being possible, a weak human mating a werewolf was the impossible made possible. I'm surrounded by werewolves, a species that shouldn't exist, yet still, I'm the puzzle among them.

Xavier stopped walking, his head turning to the left and then right, and I lifted my cheek off his shoulder. As I felt his body growing tense, I grew nervous. What would make a werewolf nervous at night, in the middle of his own woods?

"Xavier?"

"Shh."

Oh god!

He tapped my thigh, and I untangled my legs from around his waist so he could place me gently onto the ground. My eyes were wide as they looked around, but whatever Xavier was seeing or hearing, I couldn't.

"Ruby, I want you to go back to the house." He stepped away from me. "Now." He began removing his shirt and instead of backing away, I approached him. He stopped me with just a look. "Run!"

I jerked my hand away as he yelled. His voice was contorted and deeper as his shoulders hunched forward. Before I could ask what was going on, I got my answer. A werewolf barreled out of the bushes and Xavier stepped protectively in front of me, punching the wolf in the face and sending him flying backward.

Xavier began to shift, his skin tearing and ripping, his body growing in size. With it, his pants began to rip until there was nothing but shredded clothes on the ground. My body was shaking with terror, my eyes wide, and my hand clutching at my heart. My brain was telling my legs to get the hell out of here, but I couldn't.

The wolf Xavier had hit reappeared, and my legs finally started to comply with the commands coming from my brain when a second wolf appeared, its eyes on me. I stepped back and the new werewolf stepped in my direction, only to be blocked by Xavier.

Xavier howled, and I winced and covered my ears as the sound rolled up to the sky like a peal of thunder. It was like nothing I'd ever heard before, and my body shook with its force. His howl was met with two others, and I turned and ran.

I pumped my legs hard as I ran through the forest.

Branches tugged at my clothes and scratched at my skin, but with the battle I could hear behind me, the animalistic growls and snapping branches, I was more worried about Xavier. He was more capable than I was, clearly, but why weren't there wolves out patrolling or something? Were those two wolves from this pack?

Tears began rolling down my cheeks as I heard one of the wolves cry out behind me. The sound was horrific, and I prayed to any god that could hear me that Xavier would be safe.

My legs were aching and no doubt bleeding, but I couldn't stop running. I had to get back to the house and let everyone know what was happening. What the hell was even happening? Who were those wolves?

Lights from the house appeared ahead, and I began screaming. Someone must have heard Xavier. There had to be someone already outside and heading to the woods. Someone had to hear me!

"Help! Help me!"

The lights from the house grew brighter the closer I got and I swatted at the tears that were blurring my vision. This can't be happening, not now! At every turn, whenever I have a moment of joy and peace, it's immediately taken away from me. I'm sick of it!

"Help me!"

I saw the wolf a second too late.

I saw its fangs and claws just as I was slammed into a tree, as pain blossomed throughout my body. I crumpled to the ground, groaning and hugging my midsection, and a massive clawed paw was the last thing I saw before I was consumed by darkness.

Xavier

$\mathcal{M}$y fists came down hard on the island, breaking a chunk of the marble off and leaving the rest cracked. Everyone who had been speaking fell quiet as my growl rumbled through the house. My wolf was losing its mind, and I was quickly losing control.

She's gone. Ruby's gone!

"We'll find her," Natalie said, but her soft voice wasn't offering me comfort.

I started pacing back and forth, my eyes closed, as I clenched and unclenched my fists. Ruby's smile kept flashing within the darkness in my mind. I kept seeing the fascination that had been on her face only a few hours ago when she had seen my true form.

I had been worried about scaring her, but she hadn't been scared at all, not in the least. I felt like a fool for thinking she would run for the hills.

Ruby's strong, she's brave, and whoever had taken her was going to die a million deaths by my hand.

I had heard her screaming for help when suddenly the two wolves I had been fighting turned and ran. They had been nothing but a distraction. They had done their job of keeping me busy while someone else went for Ruby. I never should have told her to run back to the house without me.

"Fuck!" My fist went through the fridge, and my dad walked up to me and placed his hand on my shoulder. "We tracked the wolves far east before their scents just vanished, Dad. Her scent as well. Those wolves aren't from any pack I know, so who the fuck were they?"

He squeezed my shoulder and I held his stare as he spoke. "We have wolves out right now looking for her, so the second someone finds something, anything, we'll know. I also sent Anna to get Willow. Maybe she'll be able to do a location spell to find Ruby. We'll find her, Xavier."

I ran my hand down my face, pulling the skin taut as I looked at Natalie and Randoll, both of them sporting angry expressions. "I want her back," I told them, and Natalie nodded.

"We'll find her," Natalie replied. I could see that she too was trying to control her rage. I knew she blamed herself for everything that had happened because if it was not for her, I wouldn't have found Ruby at all.

But I could never blame her for bringing my mate into my life.

"Do you think it's the Council?" Randoll asked as he looked between my father and me. My dad shook his head.

"I don't think so," he replied, his eyes on the broken island. "This isn't the way the Council does things, but we also can't overlook them. I can reach out to my contact, but doing that means they'll learn about Ruby if they weren't the ones who took her."

I placed my elbows onto the island and began rocking back and forth. "No. We can't risk that. We'll find out who did this *when* we find Ruby."

The feeling of panic and rage I had experienced the night Ruby had almost been raped was returning with a vengeance. That night I had been there. I had been able to act swiftly.

But now I had no idea what danger she was in. I had no idea what was being done to her while we all stood around chatting.

"Maybe it's rogue wolves," Randoll suggested, and I nodded in agreement. Rogue wolves are rare but real. Most of them become mercenaries for anyone who will purchase their services, so it's possible rogues were hired to take Ruby. "My question is this, how would rogue wolves even know about her unless someone in this pack broke Dad's command to not speak of her to outsiders?"

"I'll call a meeting. I'll find out if someone here betrayed us." My dad left the kitchen and Natalie and Randoll shared a look. Disobeying my father is rare because everyone knows he can be as cruel as he can be kind.

"How are Jackson and Raven?" I asked Randoll. They were the wolves assigned patrol duty tonight. He sighed heavily. That was a bad sign.

"They're in pretty bad shape, but alive."

Natalie turned away. "I'll go to her room and find something that her energy is tied to strongly. Willow will need it."

My dad walked back into the room as he pocketed his phone and Natalie stopped in her tracks. The look on his face gave me pause, a sick feeling settling in my gut.

"They picked up her scent. Her blood was found, but there's no way to track it. Her scent started and ended where they found the blood."

I began taking deep breaths as my urge to shift grew stronger. In times of heightened emotions an accidental shift can happen, and losing my shit right now wouldn't help anyone. It wouldn't help Ruby.

They had found her blood. Those fuckers were dead men

walking! I went to walk past my dad when he grabbed my arm. He looked at me, his eyes narrowed before he looked at Randoll and Natalie as well. "Something's coming and Ruby's going to have a big part to play. We need to find her. The goddess doesn't make mistakes."

Ruby

 y bones ached as if they had all been broken and then reset and were on their way to healing. I was at a loss for why my body felt so fucked up, but I remained still until my throbbing headache eased.

I inhaled and my nose crinkled from a horrible stench.

What the hell is that?

I cracked one eye open, but surprise soon had my other eye popping open as well. Why was there a stone ceiling above me?

I bolted upright as I realized I was in a dimly lit dank cell and not my room at Xavier's house. An odd heaviness on my left leg pulled my attention and my heart started pounding harder at the sight of a chain attached to my ankle.

What the fuck is going on?

My headache returned in an unpleasant wave, and I hunched over and held my head. Images began flashing within my mind, of me running into the forest, of Xavier's wolf hitting me with his tail, of a strange werewolf attacking me and sending me flying through the air.

"Fuck," I said under my breath as all my memories returned to me, and my mouth went dry as I took a closer look at the cell I was in. There was the bed I was sitting on and an old, disgusting toilet but nothing else. With only a single window high above the bed, I was sitting on, very little light was coming into the room.

It was enough, however, for me to suddenly see someone standing in the shadows outside my cell. I swung my legs off the bed, the chain on my leg slowing me down, but I got to my feet and dragged myself forward.

"Who are you? What am I doing here?" The person didn't move or speak, and my nostrils flared. "Hey, dipshit! What the fuck am I doing here? What do you want?" The chain stopped me before I could reach the bars separating me from the creep who was watching me.

"Answer me! Let me out of this nasty-ass cell right now!"

"So, you're the human mate." My mouth slammed shut at the deep booming voice of my watcher. "I was expecting more. Even for a human, you look so fragile."

"Yeah, how about you unchain me, and you'll see what this fragile human can do, huh?"

The man chuckled, and a chill went down my spine that had nothing to do with how cold it was. My breathing became labored, and I suddenly felt overwhelming fatigue. How the hell was I going to get out of this?

Being a bitch won't help you.

I gritted my teeth at the voice in my head and did my best to straighten my spine. "Look, you've got the wrong girl okay? I have nothing, literally nothing, that anyone wants. Let me out of here, please."

"Oh, you're the right girl."

My shoulders slumped and my head fell back. "What do you want? Tell me what it is you want then."

"Oh, you'll find out soon enough. What are you?"

I frowned at that. Did I smell like a wolf or something? Because that was the only reason this person could be asking me such a stupid question. I bit my tongue to hold back my sarcastic response and tilted my head to the side.

"What do you mean? Can't you tell that I'm human?"

The man tsked. "No, you're not. No human can be mated to a wolf, and you're mated to two. You're not human, and I'm going to figure out what you are."

"Look, buddy, all of this is a shock to me as well, okay? I'm human. Just unlucky enough to be the first to be mated to a wolf…or wolves."

The shadow moved as if the person had planned on stepping into the light, but they froze. "If it was up to me, I'd kill you." I clenched my fists at my sides and I bit the side of my cheek. If this guy's plan was to scare me shitless, it was working. I couldn't believe it. At first, I had thought I was in hell being at Xavier's house, but that was a palace compared to where I found myself now. "But it's not up to me, not yet. News of a human being mated to a wolf can never get out. Weak wolves like Alpha Mathieu who think they can live peacefully with humans will never hear of this. They'll never think it's possible to bond with humans."

The man turned to leave, and the words tumbled from my lips before I could stop them. "He's going to find me you know!" He paused but didn't turn around. "Xavier is going to find me, and when he does, whoever the hell you are, you're going to be sorry! You hear me! Sorry!"

He continued walking and a door opened, blinding me. "Help! Help me!"

The door slammed shut, leaving me alone in the empty cell as I continued to scream.

Please find me, Xavier, please.

NATALIE

*W*illow hadn't been able to locate Ruby, and it had only enraged Xavier further. However, using the scratch that Xavier got on his arm from brawling with one of the strange wolves, she had been able to locate that wolf.

Xavier hadn't waited a second before he was out the door with Randoll and six others.

I was left behind to help Mathieu with creating a mental link with the entire pack to see who had gone against his command and told someone about Ruby. Creating a mind link is allowed only under specific circumstances. Alphas demand total obedience, and once an order is given it's almost impossible to disobey. But some wolves are strong enough to overpower the will of their alpha. In circumstances like this, a mind link through an Enchanted may be done.

It's taxing on an Enchanted, however, having all the thoughts and memories from the pack flowing through their minds to then be sent to the alpha. No one was guilty of talking about Ruby, though, and it left us with more questions than answers.

There was a time when the Enchanted were shunned, beaten, or killed for not being able to transform. Different is rarely accepted in the werewolf community. A she-wolf who can't transform, but can delve into the minds of others, who can see the past and get glimpses of the future, was a little too different for most werewolves.

I'm happy to have been born in a time when I don't have to live in hiding from humans *and* wolves. Would a time come when I wouldn't have to live in hiding from humans as well? Was Ruby's existence the start of a new world?

I've heard that some Enchanteds get so powerful they are almost like witches. If only I had those powers, I'd be able to find Ruby. I'd be able to break through that wall in her mind and see what lies behind it. I'm still young and my powers are still developing, so there's only so much I can do, but there is someone else who is able to do much more. So before Xavier had left, he had asked me to find the only Enchanted he knew of who could help.

Raindrops pummeled my body as I walked briskly through the street, people running in all directions to get out of the sudden downpour. I spotted my destination on the other side of the street and dashed across as lightning flashed overhead.

I pushed the door of the shop open and stepped inside, water dripping off my body and onto the wooden floor.

The shop was dark, lit by only a few candles, and the air was thick with the smell of incense. I looked around at the shelves that lined the walls, all stacked with books, jars of liquids and powders, and other mysterious objects.

"You're three minutes late," a woman said as she entered the shop through a curtain of beads at the back of the room. "At least I was right about the rain," she mumbled under her breath as she approached me and handed me a towel.

Her eyes were white, completely white, and so was her hair, which was in messy dreads and piled high on top of her head. She was shorter than me, five foot four maybe, with bracelets covering both her arms and crow's feet at the corners of her eerie eyes.

"How did you know I was coming?" I asked.

She dismissed my question with a wave of the hand and turned away. "Child, don't insult me. One day you'll be able to do the same." She pointed a finger at me over her shoulder. "You're a strong one. I can sense it. You'll possess greater powers than I." She stopped at the curtain of beads and looked back at me. "Are you coming, or do you plan on standing at my door the whole day?"

I dried my hair as much as I could as I followed her through the curtain and stepped into a very modern-looking living room. What a contrast from the dark gloomy shop! It was brightly lit and aesthetically furnished in black and white. There was even an electric fireplace.

"Um, you're Adolfa right?"

The woman nodded and took a seat before waving her hand to the sofa. "Sit. Xavier sent you, and we need to get this over with quickly." She folded her wrinkled hands together in her lap as I sat down. "Times are quickly changing, and I'll be leaving soon."

I narrowed my eyes at her. She has to be blind. There is no way her eyes look like that and she's not blind. I waved my hand. "I'm sorry, but are you blind?"

"In one sense of the term, but my inner eyes show me everything I need to see. Stop waving your hand."

My hand fell onto my lap. "Sorry. So, where are you going? You said you'll be leaving soon," I asked her, and she laughed and reclined in her chair.

"Do you know how people like us were created?"

I shook my head and then remembered she couldn't see me. "No."

"Many wolves worship our goddess, but they don't believe she really exists. Yet they've all met her through an Enchanted. Did you know that the first Enchanted was the goddess's half-human child? To meet an Enchanted is to meet the goddess. So, if we're being honest, all Enchanted are royalty. They all have divine blood."

She has to be joking right? Why had no one told me this before?

I looked down at my hands as if I could find confirmation there that what she was saying was true. I'm a descendant of the goddess? Why isn't this widely known? Enchanted are still looked down upon even now in some parts of the world. Some accept us, but others are just polite and skilled at hiding their disgust.

"I didn't know that. Why isn't this widely known? Enchanted are teased and bullied, called witches when in reality we're demigods."

She raised her hands and shook her head. "Now, now, while we do have the goddess's blood, we only have a little of it. As centuries have gone by, we've lost our power. Its potency has been diluted as our bloodline was mixed with those of normal wolves. We aren't demigods, Natalie, and werewolves have forgotten a lot. Maybe too much. And they're going to pay for their negligence. I'm not one to support the Council, but they do their best to preserve our history and our origins."

"And Ruby? You knew I was coming, so you must know about her."

A smile began to grow on her lips, an answer without words. She knew whom I was talking about. I had known it. Deep down I had known Ruby was special from the moment I had seen her. I was, however, also an expert at knowing that in this world there is no one more hated than a supernatural that is different than other supernaturals. I might not be able to see Ruby's future, but I know she'll be facing a lot of backlash for merely existing. No human I've met has ever had such a pure white aura.

"Mm, yes." Adolfa interlocked her hands under her chin, her nails long and pointed, their tips black, and I watched closely as she closed her eyes. "Young Ruby...she has her father's hair."

Her father?

I sat forward, my heart skipping a beat. Was she seeing her?

With being so caught up with everything that had been happening, I never thought to ask Ruby about her life before she had moved here. It was clear it hadn't been a life filled with rainbows and unicorns, but where had she come from?

Mathieu would have done a background check on her, surely. But as her friend, I should have asked, and for that, I felt horrible.

"Why did the goddess allow her to be mated to two wolves, and two future alphas at that? Nothing good can come from this. A human being mated to one wolf would have been bad enough. But two? This is a problem, for everyone."

"Indeed it is my child, indeed it is. But the goddess doesn't make mistakes."

I sighed with exasperation and rubbed at my forehead. "Yes, I keep hearing that, like there is something I'm missing like there is something I should know. I'm here to find out what that thing is. She was taken, Adolfa. Someone abducted her."

She nodded. "I know." She opened her eyes once more and I frowned as they began to dart frantically from left to right. "Ruby isn't the problem, Natalie." She stood up and walked over to me as she reached out and cupped my cheek.

"Then what is she?"

Her wrinkled face brightened with an almost sinister grin, and before I knew what was happening she shoved one of her fingernails into my forehead. My body went as stiff as a board and then jerked as she pressed her nail deeper.

My body grew cold, and I breathed out through my mouth, unable to move as I stared at the fog my breath created. The world around me began to fall away. She began speaking under her breath, and my eyes rolled back. My mouth slowly gaped open, and a scream was torn from my chest.

Xavier

*A*s it was daytime, transforming wasn't an option. Our senses would be heightened, but the risk was too great, so we stayed in human form as we surrounded the warehouse.

The warehouse was less than a mile away from where Ruby's blood had been found and her scent didn't go past this warehouse. Even though I was right outside, I still could not smell the unknown wolves. A wolf has never been able to block their scent so completely.

With each passing second of not having Ruby in my arms, I grew more and more aggravated. I had only just found her; we were just getting close, and now she's gone.

She's not gone forever!

I clenched my fists before looking to my left and nodding to Randoll, his signal to move forward. He nodded in response and whistled, and the wolves who had surrounded the warehouse charged in.

Yells, growls, and loud crashes could be heard as they stormed inside. While we were unable to smell these wolves, I was certain they could smell us and had been preparing for our attack. But were they as pissed off as we were? They came onto my land, our land, and took one of ours.

"Maim, not kill! Not until I have answers!" I reminded my pack.

I had to hold myself back from joining the fight, for I wouldn't be able to stop myself from killing, and we needed information. My wolf was scratching beneath my skin to be released. He was begging to take over so he could go on a rampage to find his mate.

Doing that would get me nowhere; dead men don't speak.

"We'll find her." I said under my breath, my gums tingling with the need to sink my teeth into something. "Calm down."

I entered the warehouse and inhaled the pungent smell of old iron and waste. My nose crinkled in disgust. The place was run down, but it was clear these wolves had been using it as a home, or maybe just a meeting place.

Two wolves were battling it out with four of my men, but they stood no chance. I inhaled deeply, trying to find Ruby's scent through the onslaught of smells around me, but I couldn't smell anything. She wasn't here.

"Xavier!" Randoll yelled. But I was on guard and ready for a fight. I spun around and landed an uppercut on the man who had been trying to sneak up on me.

He staggered away from me and wiped at the corner of his mouth as blood instantly bubbled to the surface. I narrowed my eyes at a deep cut on his neck and my fangs elongated. "You. You were there last night."

He smiled at me and my wolf howled so loud within my head my vision blurred. My thirst for blood had me ripping my shirt off. "Where is she?" He began removing his shirt as well and I widened my stance as he hunched forward, his nails piercing the tips of his fingers like needles. "I'll only ask once more, where is she?"

"Not here." The man growled.

He charged at me, but a gunshot echoed in the space around us. The man was thrown to the side, blood spraying as he fell to the ground.

Scanning the warehouse, I saw Randoll lower his gun. I turned back to the dying wolf, black lines spreading from the wound.

I stepped over to him. His eyes glared at me with hatred,

and I sighed and folded my arms over my chest. "I don't have time to fight with you. Tell me where she is, and I'll give you a quick death." The lines were spreading quickly, and he began to wheeze. "There is wolfsbane in that bullet. The poison will keep spreading. Speak up, and I'll help you. Who hired you to take her? Where is she?"

He started laughing and the neutral, impassive look on my face disappeared. I reached down, my hand shifting as I did so, and my claws wrapped around his throat. I picked him up, lifting the six-foot-two man off the ground as if he weighed less than Ruby before slamming him back down, the floor cracking beneath him.

Blood bubbled to his lips and spilled from the sides of his mouth and his cry pierced the silence around us as the nails on my other hand sank into his thighs, cutting through flesh and bone.

"How are you able to hide your scent?"

Harming another wolf, enemy or not, was something I hated and never took joy in doing. But in this case, they fucked with the wrong girl, and they deserved what was coming to them.

"Where is she?" I yelled and the man grew still. He was still breathing shallowly, and I bared my teeth as he began to smile.

He stuck his tongue out, and my eyes widened at the small pill on the tip. I removed my hand from his thigh and grabbed at his face, but he had already swallowed the pill. The reaction was instant as he began to shake and foam at the mouth.

I released him as the other two wolves my men had secured started foaming at the mouth as well, their hands and legs twisting in odd directions as their eyes rolled back.

"The fuck?" Randoll said under his breath, a look of surprise passing between him and the other wolves.

I saw red.

I punched a pillar to my right, breaking it in half, and the roof of the warehouse groaned almost in pain. I howled so loudly an already cracked window shattered as I stormed outside.

"Burn it down!"

My phone began ringing and every fiber in my being was telling me to throw the thing into a wall. I need her! I need her back!

Natalie was the only hope left now, and I hoped she had gotten some information from the old Enchanted I had asked her to see. If not, we'd be officially lost, with no way of finding her from this point. The first few hours of a person going missing or being taken are the most crucial. We barely have anything to go on as it is.

"Yes, Dad?" I answered.

"Xavier, what did they say?"

I sighed and placed my hand on my forehead, my temples throbbing. "Nothing. The fuckers just took some kind of pill and offed themselves. We got nothing!"

I heard something shatter in the background, and I clenched my teeth. "Then we have a serious problem."

"What is it?"

"Get back to the house."

My hold on the phone tightened, and I heard a crack as I switched it from one ear to the next. "Damn it, Dad, just say it. What is it?"

There was a long pause. The longer the silence stretched the more my body began to shake with panic. "Natalie is missing, and Adolfa is dead."

Ruby

*J*erked awake and looked around. When I realized I was still in the dreary cell, I closed my eyes and turned onto my side. I had hoped that the man in the shadows and the chain around my ankle were just a bad dream.

But as usual, I never get what I want. The universe has been dishing out shit to me since the moment I was born.

Waking up and finding Xavier watching me while I slept was something I'd pick over this any day of the week. I missed him. I missed him so much, fresh tears sprang to my eyes and threatened to fall. I squeezed my eyes closed to stop them and tried to remember what it felt like to have his warm body close to mine.

Whoever abducted me might be watching me right now, might be listening, and I wouldn't give them the satisfaction of seeing or hearing me cry. I wanted to scream at the top of my lungs, but what would that change? My hair was tangled so badly my fingers could not run through it, and I didn't need heightened senses to know that I was starting to smell funky.

None of that would be changed by my screaming and losing my voice in the process.

I wasn't sure how much time had passed since I'd been here, but I'd seen two days and one night come to an end and now it was nighttime again. I'd been sleeping nonstop, and wouldn't be surprised if at some point I'd slept through an entire day.

Am I going to die here?

I missed Natalie as well, and her perky warmth and ability to make me feel better. I felt alone, utterly alone in this place, and I was starving! I was starting to feel weak, my body in need of sustenance. Only once since I'd been here had I woken up to find bread and water inside my cell, but since then I'd had nothing to eat or drink.

'What are you?'

The shadow man's question whispered in my mind, and I took a deep breath. What I am is cursed, that's what I am. All I had wanted was to get an education, to earn my degree and pray that it would be something to change my life for the better.

Two weeks in, and the shit had hit the fan.

My stomach growled and I turned onto my other side, now facing away from the window, and my heart stopped as yet again someone was standing in the shadows. This time I remained still, too weak to get up anyway.

I couldn't see the man's face, but I could feel his eyes on me. So I stared back, my eyes blinking slowly.

"Are you hungry?"

"No, I've been eating all day. I'm kind of full, thanks."

Dumbass, of course I'm hungry!

I realized this was a different voice. It wasn't as gravelly and painful to the ear, but still deep and husky, like the voice a man has when he just wakes. I placed my hand under my cheek and narrowed my eyes.

"You're not the man from before. Are you able to tell me why I'm here or will there be someone else coming to watch me in the dark after you?"

"Something really needs to be done about your smart mouth."

Who the hell is this guy?

"Sorry, there is no cure." I sat up but left my leg with the chain on the bed while the other hung over the edge. "So, who are you? It's creepy to watch someone while they sleep."

"It's not creepy if the person I'm watching is my mate."

I tasted blood in my mouth as I bit down on my tongue when Axel stepped out of the shadows. I clenched my fists and got off the bed, dragging myself closer to the iron bars. I eyed him up and down, and my stomach turned as a sickening smirk grew on his lips.

"What the hell are you doing, Axel? What's going on?"

He buried his hands into his jeans pockets and shrugged. "Isn't it obvious?"

"No, it's really fucking not. What's going on? How are you even doing this? I thought mates couldn't hurt each other."

I couldn't believe what I was seeing. Was the man before me really Axel? It looked like him, dark clothes, dark smirk and all. It was him. I saw his eyes look down at my ankle quickly before they met my angry stare once more.

"Who told you that?" He crossed his arms over his chest. "You'd have to be my mate for that to apply."

"You just said I am your mate!"

"Be quiet, child!"

Child?

I recoiled as his yell stung my eardrums and he walked forward until he was holding onto the bars. His eyes were burning with such hatred I looked away, confused at the tightness within my chest. How can he hate me so much? He doesn't even know me.

My voice was low when I spoke, almost unrecognizable to me. "I didn't ask for this. I didn't ask for any of this."

His hands fell away from the bars and I looked at him, his face now smooth but his eyes still intense. "Neither did I, but this happened anyway, and now it will be handled. I don't want you."

"Reject me then."

His eyes lowered into slits and I held his stare the way I had in the living room days before. Silence reigned around us as we stared at each other, and I crossed my arms over my chest. His eyes followed my every move, and I arched a brow to show that I was waiting for his response.

"Reject me."

"Well, aren't you brave? I don't know what rejecting you will do to me just yet. You're human. This is unknown territory. Maybe you were created for this, to have me reject you and I get hurt instead. I have a lot of enemies who want to see me fall."

"That's not surprising." He shook his head, and I shifted my weight from one leg to the other. "You know, one wouldn't peg you for a nut job just by looking at you. Do you even hear what you're saying? For the last time, I wasn't *created*. I'm a real person!"

I stepped forward, but the chain dug into my leg, making me wince. I saw the way his face twitched as his eyes looked down to my leg, and I felt a flicker of hope. No matter how much he pretended to hate me, he was still affected by our bond.

Maybe I could play on the bond's strength, get through to him by begging. "Please, Axel, don't do this. Let me out of here, please."

His head tilted to the side as he regarded me curiously. I felt like an animal at a zoo. His eyes roamed up and down my body, and I grew self-conscious.

"You really think that will work on me, don't you?"

I frowned.

"Do you think batting your lashes and flipping your hair will get you out of this?" He held onto the bars once more. "This is real life, Ruby. Charm won't get you out of this. Xavier's weak. It's not surprising he fell for you, but I won't. You're a *human*, a weakling. You're not fit to be my mate."

His words stung me more than I expected, and I bit my tongue again to stop the tears burning behind my eyes from breaking free. "Then what will get me out of this? Tell me! Tell me what I need to do or just reject me. Reject me and be free of me then, instead of telling me over and over again how much I disgust you. You can't stand the sight of me, and that is clear. I'm not your biggest fan, either. But don't keep me down here. This won't change the fact that I'm your mate. You don't want me, but Xavier does. Let me go back to him."

His jaw visibly clenched at the mention of Xavier's name and his low growl had me stepping back. I wasn't blind, I could see the killer within his eyes. I had seen it from the first time we met.

He and Xavier are like night and day. Xavier brought the sun to my world, but Axel was darkness personified.

"No." He replied, his voice low and almost inaudible. He turned his back to me, and I stared at him. I didn't need him to like me or love me, I just needed him to let me go. I hadn't asked to be his or Xavier's mate. Why punish me like this? There had to be more to this story.

"Why are you punishing me like this? Did a human do something to you?"

He spun around. "Are you serious? What are you doing? Do you think I'm going to open up to you?" He laughed, but it held no humor. "I'll reject you soon enough, so sit tight. Do you want to know why you're here? I've been trying for years to be rid of the Blackmoon Pack. They're weak, they aren't real wolves, and they're the ones sitting on prime land while my pack has to settle for scraps. Now you've presented the perfect chance for me to strike."

I stepped back until the back of my leg hit the bed. "W-what do you mean?"

"Aww, you thought this was about you and this mate bull-shit? Sure, I can't stand the thought of you being my mate, but you, little Ruby, you just single-handedly brought down an entire pack." A sick feeling began to settle in my chest as he backed away until he was cloaked in darkness again. "You see, humans always bring destruction, and this will all be blamed on you. Let's see if Xavier loves you after that."

The door opened and he vanished through it.

I collapsed onto my bed as I hugged myself, my tears finally breaking free. My breathing started coming out in sharp gasps as I slid off the bed and onto the cold floor. No, no, what did he mean by saying I brought down the Black-moon Pack?

I looked toward the door through the iron bars and started sobbing. Whatever he's planning, Xavier won't fall for it. He won't. I pulled my knees up and rested my forehead on them, and for the first time since being in this cell, I cried until I lost all the strength in my body and fell unconscious.

LUNA CAPTURED

Luna Captured (Book 2)

https://ssbks.com/LR2

I must have been *CURSED* from birth...

...and that is becoming clearer with every passing day.

My ankles are swollen from the chains around them, my tongue feels like sandpaper, and the dripping water in the jail cell beside mine is so close, yet so far away.

For the first time in werewolf history, two wolves have the same mate.

The same woman was blessed by their goddess to be their partner for eternity, and I'm that woman.

Yeah, that's not a blessing to me...

It's bad enough I'm a human and unworthy of being a wolf's mate, but now I'm the mate to two rival wolves, two alphas-to-be.

Xavier and I have grown close...

...but *Axel Grimmwolf*, eye candy and a man no one dares stand against, is disgusted by the thought of a human being as his mate.

But even so, he lacks the strength to reject me...

So here I am, chained up in his dungeon, with no idea what Axel will do with me after he uses me to get rid of Xavier's pack.

Assuming I live that long...

I know Xavier is searching for me, but what if he doesn't find me in time?

What if this is how I'm meant to die?

https://ssbks.com/LR2

Click below to get your FREE copy of the **Luna Rising Prequel**.

https://ssbks.com/LunaPrequel

Axel

I'm next in line to be **ALPHA**

…and I'm ready for the challenge.

Focused and determined to make my father proud, I won't let *anything* get in my way.

Until the day I met **HER…**

She's a drop-dead gorgeous blonde with eyes like an aquamarine gem…and she's a witch.

But I'm a werewolf.

And some unions are **FORBIDDEN...**

That little witch has turned my world upside down.

All love comes at a cost.

But this love may cost me *everything*...

https://ssbks.com/LunaPrequel

ALSO BY SARA SNOW

THE LUNA RISING UNIVERSE

LUNA RISING SERIES (A PARANORMAL SHIFTER
SERIES)

Luna Rising Prequel (Free Download)

https://ssbks.com/LunaPrequel

Luna Rising (Book 1)

https://ssbks.com/LR1

Luna Captured (Book 2)

https://ssbks.com/LR2

Luna Conflicted (Book 3)

https://ssbks.com/LR3

Luna Darkness (Book 4)

https://ssbks.com/LR4

Luna Chosen (Book 5)

https://ssbks.com/LR5

THE BLOODMOON WARS (A PARANORMAL SHIFTER SERIES PREQUEL TO LUNA RISING)

The Awakening (Book 1)

https://ssbks.com/BW1

The Enlightenment (Book 2)

https://ssbks.com/BW2

The Revolution(Book 3)

https://ssbks.com/BW3

The Renaissance (Book 4)

https://ssbks.com/BW4

The Dawn (Book 5)

https://ssbks.com/BW5

THE VENANDI UNIVERSE

THE VENANDI CHRONICLES

Demon Marked (Book 1)

https://ssbks.com/VC1

Demon Kiss (Book 2)

https://ssbks.com/VC2

Demon Huntress (Book 3)

https://ssbks.com/VC3

Demon Desire (Book 4)

https://ssbks.com/VC4

Demon Eternal (Book 5)

https://ssbks.com/VC5

THE DESTINE UNIVERSE

DESTINE ACADEMY SERIES (A MAGICAL
ACADEMY SERIES)

Destine Academy Books 1-10 Boxed Set

https://ssbks.com/DA1-10

ENJOY THIS BOOK? I WOULD LOVE TO HEAR FROM YOU...

Thank you very much for downloading my eBook. I hope you enjoyed reading it as much as I did writing it!

Reviews of my books are an incredibly valuable tool in my arsenal for getting attention. Unfortunately, as an independent author, I do not have the deep pockets of the Big City publishing firms. This means you will not see my book cover on the subway or in TV ads.

(Maybe one day!)

But I do have something much more powerful and effective than that, and it's something those publishers would kill to get their hands on:

A WONDERFUL bunch of readers who are committed and loyal!

Honest reviews of my books help get the attention of other readers like yourselves.

If you enjoyed this book, could you help me write even better books in the future? I will be eternally grateful if you could spend just two minutes leaving a review (it can be as short as you like):

Please use the link below to leave a quick review:

http://ssbks.com/LR1

I LOVE to hear from my fans, so *THANK YOU* for sharing your feedback with me!

Much Love,

~Sara

ABOUT THE AUTHOR

Sara Snow was born and raised in Texas, then transplanted to Washington, D.C. after high school. She was inspired to write a paranormal shifter series when she got her new puppy, a fierce yet lovable Yorkshire Terrier named Loki. When not eagerly working on her next book, Sara loves to geek out at Marvel movies, play games with her family and friends, and travel around the world. No matter where she is or what she is doing, she can rarely be found without a book in her hand.

Or Facebook:
   Click Here
   https://ssbks.com/fb
   Join Sara's Exclusive Facebook Group:
   https://ssbks.com/fbgroup

Printed in Great Britain
by Amazon